RANGE PIRATE

RANGE PIRATE

Matt Stuart

Chivers Press • G.K. Hall & Co.
Bath, England   Thorndike, Maine USA

This Large Print edition is published by Chivers Press, England, and by G.K. Hall & Co., USA.

Published in 1997 in the U.K. by arrangement with Golden West Literary Agency.

Published in 1997 in the U.S. by arrangement with Golden West Literary Agency.

U.K. Hardcover ISBN 0-7451-8945-8 (Chivers Large Print)
U.K. Softcover ISBN 0-7451-8956-3 (Camden Large Print)
U.S. Softcover ISBN 0-7838-2047-X (Nightingale Collection Edition)

Copyright © 1948, 1949 by L. P. Holmes
Copyright © 1950 by L. P. Holmes in the British Commonwealth
Copyright © renewed 1975, 1976 by L. P. Holmes

First published under the title *Water, Grass, and Gunsmoke* (Doubleday, 1949) by L. P. Holmes.
An earlier version of this story appeared under the title 'Water, Grass, and Gunsmoke' by L. P. Holmes in *Giant Western* (Summer, 1948).

All rights reserved.

The characters and the incidents in this book are entirely the products of the author's imagination and have no relation to any person or event in real life.

The text of this Large Print edition is unabridged.
Other aspects of the book may vary from the original edition.

Set in 16 pt. New Times Roman.

Printed in Great Britain on acid-free paper.

British Library Cataloguing in Publication Data available

Library of Congress Cataloging-in-Publication Data

Holmes, L. P. (Llewellyn Perry), 1895–
   [Water, grass, and gunsmoke]
   Range pirate / by L. P. Holmes.
     p. cm.
   "Originally published under the title: Water, grass, and gunsmoke."
   ISBN 0-7838-2047-X (lg. print : sc)
   1. Large type books. I. Title.
[PS3515.O4448W38   1997]
813'.52—dc21   96-48189

CONTENTS

1. Ghost Legacy 1
2. Pirate Acres 19
3. Thinning Ranks 38
4. Holding the Trails 56
5. The Strange Way of Men 74
6. Devious Trails 93
7. Raid by Night 107
8. Long Hate 125
9. The Ominous Tide 146
10. Wild Night 163
11. Bitter Awakening 187
12. Crimson Hours 210
13. One Man's Faith 229

CAST OF CHARACTERS

Logan Ware had given his word to a dying man. He meant to keep it.
Dave Grande ran the Empire Saloon ... and other things.
Mize Huncutt thought he could buy into Hat ranch—with murder.
Dobe Yarnell tried treachery—then violence.
Lister Beckwith was smooth. He thought he knew an easier way.
Dub Pennymaker was getting old. But he could still lift a shotgun.
Slide Maidlie lived by the gun. He was a professional killer but nobody could buy his friendship.
Tilton Bennett knew what the law said. But he also had ideas of his own.
Loren Rudd had been fooled about her father. But when she learned the truth it was very late.

CHAPTER ONE

GHOST LEGACY

It was a thoroughly used-up horse that Logan Ware unsaddled and turned into the big cavy corral at Hat headquarters. Behind Ware lay petty treachery, a dead man, and forty miles of hard riding. Ahead of him, perhaps no further distant than the bunkhouse yonder, lay more trouble, and it was his mood to meet it now, swiftly and ruthlessly.

It was the twilight hour and all of the far-running miles of Long Valley lay cooling under a rising tide of powder-blue haze. A thread of pale smoke lifted from the chimney of the cookshack and the savory odor of frying meat came across to Ware, awakening to fresh insistence the hunger which gnawed at him.

In the growing dusk he loomed a tall, flat shape, erect and wolf-lean. Sun and wind had weathered him deeply and a life in the saddle had given him a sinewy ease and swiftness of movement that were almost pantherish. The planes of his face were flat, hard-angled, the cast of his head hawkish. His nose was bold, his eyes gray, under brows curved to a certain frowning intentness.

In him lay a blend of physical youth, mental maturity, and an unswerving honesty that had caused an old, lonely, and dying man to tender him a great and exacting trust.

Ware hung his saddle on the corral fence, spread the sweat-caked blanket across it to air, then headed for the bunkhouse, the rash purpose of his mood showing in the forward thrust of his big shoulders, the smoky turbulence of his eyes, the bleak, unyielding grimness about his mouth and chin. He filled the bunkhouse door with hard-muscled challenge.

The long narrow rectangle of the room was full of deepening shadow and the idle murmur of men waiting the call of the supper gong. On the first bunk to the left of the door Tex Fortune sprawled flat on his back, hands crossed under his head, a thin line of cigarette smoke knifing upward from his pursed lips. Opposite, perched cross-legged on his blankets, Rainy Day was at work on a horsehair bridle, head low bent against the fading light. Beyond, taking their relaxed ease, were Packy Maroon, Ed Morlan, Chain Kelsey, and Buck Trubee. But not the two Logan Ware was searching for—not Morry Seever and Spade Orcutt. Ware asked for them, the brittle harshness of his tone leaving a sudden quiet hanging.

It was Tex Fortune who finally stirred and answered. 'Not here. Town, I reckon.'

'What time did they get back from Red Mountain?'

Uneasy silence met this question. Ware rolled up slightly on his toes, piling the weight of his authority across the taut room. 'Either you don't know or you don't want to tell. If it's the last, then I damn well want to know about it. Which is it?'

'I,' murmured Tex Fortune, 'don't know. Rainy and me were out all afternoon cleaning that Eagle Rock water hole. When we came back to headquarters about an hour ago, Seever and Orcutt were heading down the town trail. That's my story, kid.'

'They wasn't here at two o'clock,' spoke up Packy Maroon. 'I was line-ridin' Bucksnort Creek. My bronc picked up a stone bruise so I came on in. I heard some heavy bellerin' over in the Punch Bowl. I caught up a fresh bronc and went over there. That best whiteface bull of ours, Old Thunder, was set to tangle with a damn red roan renegade that was all horns and bones and whang leather. I choused the renegade back into the roughs and drifted Old Thunder down to the lake meadows. Which used up the rest of the afternoon for me. I didn't see Orcutt or Seever at any time. So all I know is that they wasn't here when I came in to swap broncs, which was around two o'clock.'

Ware didn't push the question any further. He'd learned enough to give him a casual approximation of time. It wasn't too important. This questioning had been more of a breaking release of some of the cold anger which rode him than anything else. His mood was to hit out, hurt, smash things.

They were a tough outfit, this Hat crew. Hamp Rudd had deliberately picked them that way, saying that he wouldn't give a thin damn for a crew that didn't have plenty of bark on it. Which was all right while Hamp Rudd was alive and there was no question in the mind of any man as to who owned every acre of Hat range and every cow under the Hat brand.

But Hamp Rudd was dead now, and the reins were in Logan Ware's hands and things were breaking and stirring all through Long Valley. There were things about Hamp Rudd's legacy which only Ware knew. But there were other things which hard, tough, self-centered men might guess at and, feeling no allegiance to a dead man, begin to weaken under the bite of greed. These were times when it was difficult to guess who could be fully trusted. Treachery had struck through Spade Orcutt and Morry Seever. Where, Logan Ware wondered, might the next evidence of it show?

The mellow jangle of the cookshack gong broke through the poised silence. Ware turned and went out, the crew drifting after him. They had already washed up so went on into the cookshack while Ware paused outside to scrub the worst of the dust and grime of ridden miles from hands and face.

Tex Fortune alone lingered beside Ware. Tex said, 'You didn't find the girl at Harte

City.' It was a statement, not a question. Ware turned a dripping face. 'How did you know?'

'Because she's in Canyon, right now. Spider Fell brought word last evening that she was there and wanting to see you. The boys are wonderin' what she intends to do about things.'

'I wouldn't know,' growled Ware through the folds of a busy towel. 'After what I just came out of I wouldn't know what anybody intends to do. Except myself. I got my own trail figured.'

'Something sure put rough edges on you,' murmured Tex. 'What's the answer, kid?'

Tex Fortune was the oldest member of the crew, with silver beginning to edge his dark hair. He was lean and leathery and soft-voiced, but tough as a twisted juniper. If trust could be placed in any member of the crew, Tex came closest to justifying it.

'I was on my way back from Harte City,' explained Ware. 'I took the old Guenoc trail, swinging past the north end of Red Mountain. Thought I might run across Seever and Orcutt and bring them on home with me. I don't see Orcutt and Seever but I do bump into that 'breed, Ute Rhyde. There's a stranger with him and they're drifting twenty head of Hat cows toward Big Sage. Rhyde wastes no time going for his gun. See here?' Ware touched a finger to the side of his corded, sun-darkened neck, where ran a livid line as though a hot iron had brushed.

'That close Rhyde came,' Ware went on. 'I made sure he didn't get a second try. The other hombre was slow and I got him through the shoulder. He was plenty sick and scared and glad to talk. He told me him and Ute Rhyde had bought the cows off two men that Rhyde seemed real friendly with. He claimed he didn't know their names but he described them to me. And he described Seever and Orcutt—perfect.'

Tex swore softly. 'I wondered why they were so long ridin' that Red Mountain circle. They should have been back two days ago.'

'This stranger said Rhyde paid two hundred dollars for those twenty cows. That's pretty damn cheap beef, Tex, though it ended up costin' Rhyde a few more years of misspent life. I drifted the cows back to Red Mountain before I came on in. Right after I eat I'm headin' for Canyon. I want to see what Mr Seever and Mr Orcutt have to say for themselves.'

Logan Ware hung up the towel, combed his damp, heavy shock of black hair with his fingers.

Tex asked, 'You want I should let the rest of the crew in on the story?'

Ware turned toward the cookshack door, from which yellow lamplight was now glowing. Over his shoulder he said curtly, 'I don't give a damn. The snakes, it seems, are beginning to crawl out from under the leaves. I'd just as soon have 'em all where I can see 'em.'

It was a silent meal, soon over with. Smoky Atwater, the cook, spoke once. 'You give Logan the message Spider Fell brought, Tex?'

Tex nodded. 'Yeah, Smoky.'

There was deep hunger in Ware and he was still at the table when the rest had finished and left. Smoky Atwater leaned against the table.

'You goin' to Canyon to see that girl, Logan?'

Smoky was a patient old fellow who had been with Hat for many years. Ware said, 'I reckon. Why?'

'There's been talk,' said Smoky, 'driftin' this way and that way. About the girl figgerin' on handin' out Hat range like it was grub on a platter. You believe that?'

'I've heard such talk,' admitted Ware. 'Say she does. You wouldn't like that?'

'Not much I wouldn't!'

'Why?'

'Hamp Rudd was a tough old rooster,' said Smoky. 'He had his faults, but who ain't got some? But Hamp put in a lifetime makin' Hat what it is today. You know and I know why he did it. Mostly for his girl, who he'd never seen. Now, if she's playin' with the locoed idee of bustin' Hat up into chunks an' handin' it over to a flock of lyin' tin-horns like Mize Huncutt an' Dobe Yarnell an' Lister Beckwith, somethin' oughta be done about it.'

Logan Ware spun a cigarette into shape, then looked up at Smoky, the hardness about his eyes relaxing a little. 'Let you in on something, Smoky,' he said softly, 'if you won't tell.'

Smoky leaned forward anxiously. 'Won't tell a word, boy. Swear it.'

Ware's smile was faint. 'Like you say, Hamp Rudd was a lot of man. And he thought of that angle and provided for it. Loren Rudd won't give any of this ranch away.'

'Gospel?'

'Gospel.'

'Boy—I feel good! Here, lemme get you another cup of java.' Smoky started for his stove again, but Ware waved him off.

'Had plenty, Smoky. Now I got some more ridin' to do.'

Ware went out and headed straight for the corrals. Twilight had gone and the full soft dark of early night lay over the valley. Ware stood by the corral gate, smoking out his cigarette before letting himself into the corral and shaking out a rope. The cavy herd gave back, crowding before Ware's slow-striding advance, and when they broke and whirled under the faint light of the first stars there was the pale flash of a buckskin that Ware wanted. The loop fell true and when it tightened the buckskin followed docilely through the gate. Ware had smoothed the blanket and tossed his saddle into place when Tex Fortune came quietly up beside him.

'Nothing tougher sometimes, kid, than to carry the load a dead man leaves. Hamp Rudd got no thanks. You'll get less. And what's twenty cows, after all? Not worth the chance of stoppin' a slug.'

Ware caught the cinch, threaded the latigo, and dug a knee into the buckskin's ribs as he set up. 'The twenty cows don't count so much, no. But the idea does. If Seever and Orcutt get away with it, there'll be others who'll try.'

'There'll be others anyhow,' drawled Tex. 'You'll be just one man tryin' to watch a dozen trails at the same time. An' it can't be done.'

A sharp edge came into Ware's tone. 'Just one man, Tex?'

Tex swore softly. 'Don't count on me.'

'I am, though,' said Ware evenly. 'On you and Rainy Day, and I hope, on Packy Maroon. And Smoky, of course. The others—well, they'll jump the way they jump, and get whatever is coming to them according to the kind of cards they call for.'

'Ideals,' growled Tex, 'never got a man anything. You can't spend 'em over a bar, you can't buy grub with 'em. Only a damn fool has ideals.'

'Call it what you want, Tex, but you don't take a man's wages, eat his grub, and ride with the pride of his outfit in you while he's alive, and then turn around after he's dead and help slice to pieces the thing he built. Especially when you know the hope he put into the building. No, Tex—you don't do a thing like that and still go on living with yourself. Not if you're more than half a man. And you are.'

Ware turned the stirrup, stepped up, and spun the buckskin away in a stretching lope.

Tex Fortune stared after him. 'I hope you see more in me than I see in myself, kid,' he muttered. 'I hope you see it and that it is really there. Right now I'm not so sure...'

The buckskin was fresh and full of run, an easy-gaited horse, which, combined with the relaxation a wash and a full meal had brought, enabled Ware to let some of the burden of fatigue slide away from his loosened shoulders.

Word that Loren Rudd was in Canyon had startled Ware and in large part wiped away the disappointment he had known in not finding her in Harte City. The fact that she wanted to see him held a thread of hope, too. Maybe there was reason to be found in her, after all.

Ware had heard his share of the same talk which Smoky Atwater had referred to. And while it hardly made sense, it could not be wholly discounted in light of the attitude the girl's mother had taken down through all of Hamp Rudd's empty, lonely years. Maybe the mother had sold the daughter on the same views. Well, he'd know about that as soon as he'd had a chance to talk to her.

But first there was something else to be taken care of—the little matter of twenty Hat cows, and the men who had driven them off and sold them for a miserable two hundred dollars. A thread of the old bleak tautness came back to Ware. Morry Seever and Spade Orcutt. If they had stopped in Canyon, he'd find them.

The slope was downward all the way to the lake and the buckskin chopped out the miles like a free-running ghost. Nearing the water, the damp fresh breath of it came to Ware and he thought of how Hamp Rudd had prized it. Sunrise Lake, Hamp Rudd had called it, and he liked to stand out in front of headquarters and watch the first rays of the sun reflect up from it in a blaze of ruddy light.

The heart of Hat range, that lake, the foundation upon which Hamp Rudd had built all the rest. With it he was a king. Without it, a question mark. He had liked to ride around it, watching Hat cows filing down the trails to drink, or grazing across the marshy meadows. He liked the stretches of tules along the shore where the ruby-winged blackbirds spread their bright, silver-bell trilling. He liked the haunting plaintiveness of killdeer crying and, when the wild fowl would gather in the fall and spread curved wings against the sky, Hamp Rudd would spend hours watching.

The day before he died Hamp Rudd rode a final circle around Sunrise Lake and then, white and weary of face, called Logan Ware to his bedside and told him what he must do. There had been certain documents drawn up and signed in Hamp's bold but now shaky hand, and Doc Abbey had witnessed them.

At the end Hamp Rudd had said, 'I can trust you, Logan. But you're the only one I'm sure of. Do your best, boy. You know what my hopes were. If you can somehow make them come true, where I couldn't myself, I know there'll be some kind of reward for you.'

That was how it had happened and Logan Ware never failed to recall it all and think on it whenever he rode past Sunrise Lake. He thought of it now as the smooth-running buckskin shied slightly when a startled killdeer fluttered up close beside and sent its plaintive crying through the dark. So the bleak mood of purpose deepened in him and held him all the way on across the valley miles until the lights of Canyon lifted out of the blackness ahead.

Ware drifted the buckskin to a stop opposite the end of the row of poplar trees which marked the east side of Lake Street. Canyon was quiet, almost too quiet. A full moon was now crawling up through a tangle of summer clouds beyond the crest of Shaggy Mountain, but the poplars walled off this light and made of the street a lane of ragged darkness which the yellow glow of lamplight in window and open doorway seemed unable to probe. At the far end of the street the sprawling mass of the Valley House Hotel dominated the town.

Ware could not have explained what it was that caused him to rein up here. He had heard nothing. Yet he swung the solid bulk of his shoulders forward in instinctive challenge and his glance ran all along the street in an alert probing. In the end he sensed, rather than saw, the slight shift of movement under the poplars in front of Jake Farwell's store.

With smooth swiftness Ware stepped from the saddle and his spurs clanked softly as his boot heels bit into the dust of the street. He gave the buckskin an open-handed slap on the flank and the horse obediently swung over to the hitch rail which ran between the poplar trees.

Ware heard a muttered curse that held a betraying hoarseness of tone, and the smile that pulled at his lips was thinly mirthless. The skulker under the poplars no longer had him as a mounted target against the stars.

'You should have made up your mind, Frog,' mocked Ware. 'Mize Huncutt will give you hell for muffing this chance. But my patience has run out. Make it now, Frog—or get out of Long Valley for good.'

While speaking, Ware had been moving in, using the bulk of the buckskin as a shield. One long, swift stride carried him clear of the horse and close to the bole of a poplar. There he paused for a moment, silent, letting the still, deadly strain build up. Finally he said, 'Still waiting, Frog? Why?'

Again sounded that hoarse curse, hard and strangled now. In it was all of a man's baffled fear and frustration. And words, heavy with hate. 'You got somethin' ridin' on your shoulder, Ware. Maybe it's luck. Maybe it's the ghost of Hamp Rudd. But it won't be there forever!'

Then the speaker was gone, heavy-footed through the night. Ware waited until he heard the creak of saddle leather, the lunging grunt of a cruelly spurred horse and the fading rattle of hoofs.

He stepped onto the long, low porch of the store building and had started along it when a door at the far end opened to let out a blare of yellow light. Then this light was blocked off by the burly figure of Mize Huncutt, who was looking and listening. Noiseless as a shadow, Ware flattened against the black wall. Huncutt came a few strides along the porch and called in guarded tones, 'Any sign of him yet, Frog?'

When there was no answer, Huncutt called again. 'Frog—hey, Frog!'

Nothing came back from the night and Huncutt cursed, then stamped back through the door and closed it behind him. Logan Ware thought of what Tex Fortune had said. One man to guard a dozen trails. More than a dozen, Tex—a lot more . . .!

The door at which Mize Huncutt had appeared led to the law office of Tilton Bennett. This took in all one corner of the building with two windows facing Lake Street and a third the alley which ran off the street at right angles. The shades were drawn over all three of these and Ware gleaned nothing as he passed, beyond an indistinguishable murmur of voices.

He went on, quick striding through the night, aiming for the swinging half doors of the Empire. He stepped through, put his shoulders to the wall, and looked over the room. He spotted Morry Seever and Spade Orcutt immediately. They were at a far table, playing stud poker with Tomlin, the house man, and two other riders.

There was a cribbage board lying on a vacant table and Ware caught this up as he went by. It was of heavy, hard wood and Ware balanced it in spread fingers. Orcutt was on one side of the stud table, Seever on the other. Ware came up in back of Orcutt, who had just turned over his hole card to show the third of three tens and was reaching out to drag in the pot.

Ware said, 'Glad to see you've been winning, Orcutt. For I want two hundred dollars from you and Seever.'

Orcutt grunted, came half out of his chair, then settled back again. Across the table Morry Seever's thin, dark face jerked up and his eyes went blank and hard. Seever was the quicker mind of the two and the deadlier gun hand. Ware swung his right hand a trifle behind him.

Spade Orcutt, heavy, shambling, blunt-featured, twisted his head and looked up. 'Oh, hello, Ware,' he blurted. 'What you talkin' big money for? This ain't that kind of a game. Just a little straight stud, two-bit limit. Ordinary cow hand's delight, you know. Morry an' me can't afford anything steeper.'

Ware let him talk, bleak anger deepening in him all the time. Orcutt's clumsy babble wasn't fooling anybody and Morry Seever knew it. So now, taut and watchful, Seever droned, 'What two hundred dollars you talkin' about, Ware?'

'Why,' said Ware, 'the two hundred dollars Ute Rhyde paid you and Orcutt for twenty head of—'

The legs of Seever's chair squealed under the violence of the backward shove he gave to it. And as Seever came lunging up his hands were a reaching blur as they stabbed toward his guns. That was when Ware threw the cribbage board.

He was too close to miss and the heavy wood spatted as it caught Seever just above the left eye. There was a spurt of crimson and Seever fell back across his chair, which upset, letting Seever down on the floor with a crash.

Spade Orcutt was slow-witted and he had turned renegade cow thief against the very outfit he had worked for—but he was not a coward. He would have reached for his gun and taken his chances if Ware hadn't got there first, jerking the weapon from under Orcutt's clawing fingers while holding Orcutt trapped against the table by shoving his chair hard against the backs of his legs.

Once he had Orcutt's gun, Ware tossed it across the room, pulled the chair back, and said, 'Two hundred dollars, Spade. That money belongs to Hat. I'm taking it away from you—the hard way.'

He ripped a rigid forearm against the side of Orcutt's bull neck, staggering him. And when Orcutt, still reeling, tried to come fully around, Ware nailed him on the jaw with a punch that came clear up from his heels. Spade never did recover from that one. Ware hammered him around the table while Tomlin and the other two players cursed and scrambled as they tried to get out of the way. Dave Grande, who owned the Empire, came around the end of the bar and stood watching, his pale face impassive, while Logan Ware cornered Spade Orcutt and chopped him down with winging fists.

It had been short, savage, and wickedly complete. Morry Seever hadn't moved after hitting the floor. Spade Orcutt wasn't out, but he was helpless. Ware stood over him, panting a little, blood trickling down his lips from the single clumsy blow Orcutt had landed.

'I ought to kill you,' Ware rapped thinly. 'Any cow thief deserves that. And you and Seever are the worst and lowest of the breed. Because you stole from the outfit you were riding for. Yeah, I ought to kill you, but I'm remembering that once you were one of us. But I'm taking the two hundred dollars. Where is it?'

Orcutt fumbled, thumbing a wad of crumpled bills from a pocket. Ware smoothed and counted them. 'Only half,' he said remorselessly. 'Where's the rest?'

Orcutt nodded his battered head toward Morry Seever. Ware stepped around to Seever, rolled him over, paid no attention to the blood running from the savage gash above Seever's eye. In the pocket of Seever's shirt he found the other hundred.

Ware straightened up and met Dave Grande's impassive stare. 'Two hundred stinking dollars, Grande,' said Ware. 'For that they double-crossed their own outfit. Anything you want to say about it?'

Dave Grande shook his head. 'Not a damn thing. Your cats, they were. You skinned 'em. That's good enough for me, Ware.'

Ware nodded as he pocketed the money. 'A word you can pass along to all who are interested, Grande. Hat is just as tough as it was when Hamp Rudd was alive. If shootin' is called for in the future, Hat will be doing its share.'

Complete silence followed Logan Ware as he went out of the Empire into the night.

CHAPTER TWO

PIRATE ACRES

The meeting in Tilton Bennett's office had begun to go a little flat. The issue had been gone over half a dozen times and no real answer could be reached, it seemed, until Logan Ware showed up. On this the girl was insistent, to the disgruntlement of the men present. Mize Huncutt and Dobe Yarnell showed their impatience plainly, but Lister Beckwith and Tilton Bennett were smoother, more adept at masking their feelings. This, perhaps, was because Lister Beckwith was much the younger and he was watching the girl with deepening admiration, while Bennett, heavy and gross of body and face, had the benefit of his legal training behind him and so was used to delay.

Loren Rudd was wearing the same trim gray traveling suit she had had on when she stepped off the stage in Canyon the previous afternoon. There was a touch of dainty frilled white at the throat and wrists. Her hair was thick and heavy and tawny, her eyes a clear and faultless gray. She was lithe and trim but physically sturdy. Her face and throat were warm with soft sun tan. A certain studied severity lay in the expression about her mouth.

She stirred restlessly and said, 'There is no need of waiting further tonight, gentlemen. Logan Ware isn't going to show up. He wasn't at the ranch when my message was delivered last evening, and probably hasn't returned yet. We'll have to wait until tomorrow and hope he shows up then.'

Dobe Yarnell cleared his throat harshly. 'Why wait for Ware at all? We know he won't agree. I say the thing to do is go ahead, draw up the rightful settlements according to law, and then let Ware make the best of it.'

The girl shook her head. 'No. You admit yourself that in such a case Logan Ware would fight. And any further fighting is the one thing above all that I want to head off. Enough blood has been spilled through the past history of the Hat ranch. The rest of it must be settled amicably. So it is necessary that I see Logan Ware, discuss things with him, and make him understand my wishes in the matter.'

Tilton Bennett stirred his gross bulk and said in that thick moist voice of his, 'I'm afraid I must agree with Yarnell, Miss Rudd. I'm afraid you'll find you can do nothing with Ware. In the end he'll have to be convinced the hard way.'

The girl stood up. 'Perhaps. But I will know that at least I have tried my way. Now I will say good night, gentlemen.'

She started for the door and Lister Beckwith jumped to accompany her. That was when the knock sounded.

Mize Huncutt was closest to the door. He slipped the latch. Logan Ware stepped in. One corner of his mouth was slightly puffed and bruised, with a stain of blood not completely wiped away. Somehow the big, dark spirit of the night clung to him, a turbulence of thought and manner which ran all across the room and brought Dobe Yarnell up and alert and forward-leaning, while Tilton Bennett began an uneasy stirring.

Mize Huncutt said, 'Glad you showed up, Ware. We been expecting you.'

'So I noticed when I hit town,' retorted Ware coldly. 'You had Frog Shefflin waitin' out under the poplars. You're a poor hand at pickin' tough ones, Huncutt. Frog just thought he was salty. When I told him to make it now or clear out of Long Valley for good, he hit leather and rode. If you don't quit throwin' these tinhorn gun fighters at me, I'm going to lose my patience complete and suggest you carry the smoke yourself.'

There was a crafty solidity to Mize Huncutt not easily disconcerted. 'What's Frog Shefflin got to do with it?' he asked glibly. 'You're talkin' in circles, Ware, and I don't know what it's all about.'

Ware looked him up and down in blunt contempt. 'You lie,' he said flatly, 'as clumsy as you scheme.'

Ware turned to the girl. 'I'm Logan Ware,

ma'am. They told me up at the hotel that I'd find you here. You're probably sick to death of the company of this crowd of fine and lovely birds. Not everybody can stand 'em. They pack a scavenger smell. Shall we head back to the hotel? We can talk in private there.'

He threw the words with an almost willful recklessness and the impact of them laid a blaze of anger across Lister Beckwith's darkly handsome face and brought Dobe Yarnell completely out of his chair. Ware laughed at them, the current of his rash recklessness rising. 'If the lady wasn't present this would be a good time to settle the answer all around. Not often that I get all you snakes together in one basket.'

Tilton Bennett said, 'Please—everybody! Ware, Miss Rudd has certain things she wants to tell you. It was her suggestion that we all be present. Suppose we let the lady have her say.'

Ware swung his glance to the girl. 'Is that right?'

She nodded.

Ware shrugged. 'I'm listening.'

The harsh abruptness of Ware's tone and manner sent a flush across her cheeks, built a slight blaze in her eyes. She waited until Dobe Yarnell had settled back into his chair and Lister Beckwith returned to his. Mize Huncutt took one over against the far wall. Only Logan Ware remained standing, watching the girl.

It was in that thick, tawny hair and her gray

eyes, he thought, that the physical resemblance to her father was most apparent. Her mouth puzzled him. It was soft and red above a gently rounded chin and seemed fashioned for laughter and brightness rather than the disciplined severity it now reflected. She would, he decided, be difficult to influence. Another thing. There was a definite thread of melody in her voice, strangely sweet, when she did finally speak.

'Mr Ware. I know that Hampton Rudd put great store in your integrity and faithfulness where his interests were concerned. Let us say there is something almost admirable in your continued faithfulness since Hampton Rudd's death. But the fact remains that in Hampton Rudd's will I am named sole heir to all his properties and possessions and it is my wish to right certain injustices that took place in years past. With your knowledge of Hat affairs you can be of great help to me in clearing up these matters.'

It's true, thought Ware. Her mother sold her a foolish bill of goods and she intends to go through with it. He stirred restlessly. 'These so-called injustices, Miss Rudd—what are they?' he asked.

'Parts of Hat range were pirated from others. I intend to return those portions to their rightful owners.'

'You can't mean that!'

'I do mean it. I want no stolen acres in

my inheritance.'

'Suppose, Miss Rudd, I told you there were no stolen acres in Hat range?'

'I'm afraid I couldn't believe that.'

Ware let his glance run around the room. All four of the other men present were watching him, with triumphant mockery in their eyes. Ware said softly, 'Lady, you sure have been sold a phony bill of goods. Well, while I'm foreman of Hat there won't be one inch, let alone one acre, of Hat range parceled out to anybody, least of all to this crowd of slickery coyotes, chomping their lying jaws for a taste of Hat property. That is the way it's going to have to be, Miss Rudd.'

'In that case,' the girl said evenly, 'I have no other choice than to discharge you. Effective immediately, you are no longer foreman of the Hat ranch.'

Lister Beckwith hit his feet, exclaiming triumphantly, 'That does it! You hear what Miss Rudd says, Ware? You're through—fired! How about it, Tilton?'

Tilton Bennett crossed his hands on his bulging paunch and smiled smugly. 'It would seem so, Lister—it would seem so.'

'I guess, Ware,' put in Mize Huncutt, 'you can leave now. You're no longer concerned.'

Ware looked them over again, and again his cold, scathing laugh rang. 'Nothing I like better than to throw a jolt into you crooks. Why, you haven't even started on a ride that is awful long and will get tougher by the mile. You see, I'm still foreman of Hat—and Miss Rudd can't fire me. Oh, I can prove that to her, and I will. There's so much you hombres don't know. Not even Mr Tilton Bennett, who poses as the fountainhead of all legal wisdom. Do we have our little talk alone tonight, Miss Rudd—or tomorrow?'

The girl stared at him, her face a mirror of jumbled and baffled emotion. Preposterous as this big, rugged cowboy's words were, there was a ring of confidence in them that could not be discounted. 'You mean,' she stammered, 'that even though I'm the legal owner of Hat ranch, I can't—discharge you?'

In that instant her guard was down and Logan Ware saw that behind her poise, behind her determination, she was still a youngster, barely past her majority, trying to handle a business affair so big that it half frightened her, and that concerned a number of angles of which she was not entirely sure. Despite a previously formed determination to thoroughly dislike and mistrust her, Ware could not help feeling sorry for her now, so his tone gentled slightly as he said, 'It really is that way. I want to help you in any way that will benefit your true interests. I wouldn't lie to you.'

For a long moment she stared into his eyes. Then she nodded. 'Very well. We'll talk this over, alone.' Her glance swung around the room. 'I'll see you other gentlemen again.'

Ware opened the door for her. Lister Beckwith got to his feet and started to follow, but found Ware in front of him.

'Didn't you hear what the lady said, Lister?' Ware drawled mockingly. 'She said—alone. That means just her and me.'

He stepped out behind the girl, closed the door, took her arm. The moon had climbed high, thrusting back the shadow of the poplars, making a silver river of the street. A night wind, coming down off Shaggy Mountain, crisped the air and touched the nostril with the balsam scent of timber slopes.

The girl was silent as they moved up toward the hotel. The top of her tawny head was just even with Ware's shoulder. She walked lithely, with a free, light grace.

'You should see this moonlight on Sunrise Lake—your lake,' drawled Ware. 'One of the world's prettiest sights. I've known your father to sit up half the night, just looking at it.'

She did not answer, just quickened her step.

They were almost even with the last poplar tree when a single hoarse word whipped across the night.

'Ware!'

Logan Ware's reaction was catlike, explosive. He literally leaped for the shelter of that last poplar trunk, carrying the girl with him. The thrusting drive of his hand forced her close against the rough-barked bole of the tree, half crouched. They made it barely clear of the slug that ripped across the side of the tree, showering splinters of bark.

Over past the end of the hotel the blare of the gun had split the night wide open, the flame of it blooming redly, then winking out. But Ware had marked the spot and he had his own gun free and smashing out roaring echoes as he swung clear of the tree and raced for the spot where the treacherous shot had flamed.

The hostile gun flamed a second time, a third. Ware drove lead in return, searching the blackness about the spot; to the right of it, to the left, not wide but close in, then center and low—low!

He heard the hoarse, disbelieving gasp of a man hard hit and the final spurt of flame from the hostile gun was low to the earth, the hungry lead from it flying wild. Then Ware was over the black, sprawled figure.

'Frog!' he gritted. 'You rotten whelp! You might have hit that girl!'

Frog Shefflin did not seem to hear him. Frog was mumbling something, words ragged and choked in his throat. 'Ridin' on your shoulder, Ware. Luck! For I missed you—every—damn—shot!'

Then Frog stiffened and was utterly still.

For a long moment or two the town of Canyon lay breathlessly silent. Then came the rush of startled, excited men, with shouted questions flying back and forth. Stubby

Hoffmeyer, who owned the Valley House Hotel, was first on the scene, running the length of the porch and vaulting the rail, stumbling and falling to hands and knees, then scrambling up with mumbled curses and wheezing query.

'Where—who....?'

'Over here, Stubby,' answered Ware harshly.

Stubby recognized his voice. 'Logan! You hit?'

'No. I'm all right. But Frog Shefflin—he's done.'

Tilton Bennett's law-office door had been one of the first to slam open and Mize Huncutt, Dobe Yarnell, and Lister Beckwith were among the first to arrive, with the paunchy lawyer trailing. The Empire Bar had completely emptied, with Dave Grande among the milling, pushing crowd.

Somebody scratched a match, bent to look at Frog Shefflin's sprawled figure, and the mutter of identity ran from lip to lip. A voice said, 'Don't look like Frog had much chance.'

Logan Ware whirled, shoved through the crowd toward the voice. 'You again, eh, Huncutt? Want to push this thing further, maybe?'

Ware located Huncutt, drove against him, trampled on his toes, pushed him back, roughed him with word and action. 'Your man, Shefflin was,' he taunted, a wicked edge in his voice. 'Your man, Huncutt. You put him after me. What's the matter, afraid to make a try yourself? Come on, you damn chunk of slime—have a try! Don't always buy your dirty work done for you. What's the trouble, Huncutt—where's your nerve?'

It was raw, savage treatment which Ware handed out to Mize Huncutt, the challenge brittle and dripping with contempt. But Huncutt wanted none of Ware at this moment. He knew that the first hostile move he made he'd be down beside Frog Shefflin. For at this time Ware was a razor-keen knife, poised at Huncutt's throat.

Despite the fact that the night was chilling up, a smear of sweat oozed down Huncutt's face and shame over what he was taking but dared not resent burned like raw acid in him. He kept on backing away, wordless.

Ware turned and left him, the sarcasm in his mirthless laugh as cutting as a whiplash. The crowd shifted around and around, irresolute, not fully understanding. It was Stubby Hoffmeyer who finally spoke.

'Frog's been makin' war talk for some time, lookin' ugly and hinting what he intended to do. Seems he climbed into a saddle too rough for him.'

'He was waitin' under the poplars when I first hit town tonight,' said Ware. 'He couldn't quite wangle the nerve to start it then. I told him to get out of Long Valley. He left town, but sneaked back, hung out here in the shadow, and opened up. I was seein' Miss Rudd to the hotel. He might have hit her. That's the story. Anybody want to question it?'

Stubby Hoffmeyer said, 'He had it comin.' I'm glad he didn't hit you, Logan.'

One more of the few I can depend on, thought Logan. He said, 'Thanks, Stubby.' Then he headed back to that end poplar, the crowd making silent way for him.

He found Loren Rudd almost as he had left her, crouched against the tree. He took her by the arm and said, 'That was pretty rough business. I'm sorry you had to see it.'

Her voice was small and dry and strained. 'He—that man—he's dead? You—killed him?'

'That's the way it shapes up. Let's get out of here.'

She moved mechanically, letting him guide her steps toward the hotel. Under his hand she was trembling, not steadily, but in little shuddering starts. She stumbled slightly on the lower step of the porch. Ware's hand tightened, steadying her.

She gave a little gasp of relief when they moved from the dark shadow of the porch into the light of the hotel entrance. Like, thought Ware, a child who had been terrified by the night, finally moving into security.

She tugged free of his grip, moved away from him, turning to look at him with wide, shocked eyes.

'You,' she said again, 'killed that man. I saw you—I heard you. You—killed him!' She was accusing him, from the depths of a vast repulsion.

'He would have killed me, if he could,' reminded Ware. 'He tried—first. He didn't miss you very far.'

The obvious truth of this seemed lost on her. 'You killed him,' she said again.

Then she whirled and ran, across the hotel parlor and to the stairway beyond, as though she were fleeing from some sort of demon. There would be, Ware realized, no confidential talk with her this night.

Stubby Hoffmeyer came in, his bald head shining under the light of the hanging lamp. His round, rosy face was sober. He said bluntly, 'Mize Huncutt is the one really responsible, Logan.'

Ware nodded. 'I know. He's been needlin' Shefflin my way for a long time. Afraid to try it himself.'

Stubby shook his head. 'No, not afraid, Logan—not exactly that. Mize is a schemer. If possible he never lets his right hand know what his left is doing. He likes to direct the rough currents in the stream while he floats comfortably in a quiet eddy. You think it is all worth it, boy?'

'What do you mean?'

Stubby pursed his lips, squinted his eyes. 'Trying to hold certain things together. You'll get no thanks.'

This, thought Ware, was what Tex Fortune had told him. He shrugged. 'A man leaves a trust with you, Stubby. You do the best you can.'

Ware went out and down the street, which had cleared and quieted again. He got his buckskin bronc and led it over to Dub Pennymaker's livery stable. Nobody was around so Ware took care of the animal himself, unsaddling it and turning it into a box stall. He pulled a couple of armfuls of wild timothy from the hay chute and heaped it in the manger. The buckskin began chomping hungrily.

From the stable Ware cut back across the street, went down the alley past Tilton Bennett's now dark and silent law office, then on out across the moonlit open beyond. Soon there was a split picket fence and a garden gate which creaked slightly as he opened it and went through. The cottage in front of him looked dark until Ware went down the walk beside it. Then there was light gleaming in a kitchen window.

Ware knocked softly and inside sounded a muffled bark, admonished to silence by a gentle feminine voice. The door opened to disclose a slim, dark-haired, piquant-faced girl in gingham.

'Hello, Midge,' said Ware. 'Pretty late, I reckon. But I'd like to sit down for a couple of minutes with real folks.'

Midge Sutton said, 'Don't be an idiot. Early or late, it never makes any difference. You know that, Logan.'

A beautiful setter dog, white with red-gold ears, pushed past the girl, flagged tail waving, to thrust a moist and friendly nose into Ware's hand. Ware bent low, cupped his hands under the dog's ears, wrestled the handsome head gently from side to side. 'Speck,' he murmured. 'Old son of a gun!'

The dog rumbled deep in its throat, loving it.

Beyond the kitchen table, capable hands and forearms white with flour as she worked over a bread pan, Mother Sutton said, 'He knew your step, Logan. He's tired of Midge and me, lonesome for the company of a man.'

Ware moved to a chair and settled into it wearily, dropping his hat on the floor. The dog laid its head on his knee. 'Steve still over at Lockeford?' Ware asked.

Midge said, 'He'll be home tomorrow. His new double hitch of wagons has finally arrived from the East.'

Ware looked at her. 'Steve's a lucky whelp.'

Midge colored. She had always been a shy, birdlike little soul. As Midge Parks, an orphan, she had had a tough row, running a little eating house. Her marriage to big, hearty Steve Sutton, who ran a freight route between Canyon and Lockeford, at rail's end over past Shaggy Mountain, had always been rich proof to Logan Ware that some things, at least, were right with the world.

Mother Sutton, gray-haired, kindly, said quietly, 'I heard shots, Logan. What were they about?'

Midge, who had picked up a bit of sewing, now let it drop in her lap, her hands idle while she watched Ware, noting the shadow in his eyes, the taut bleakness about his lips, the overall sag of weariness which seemed to pull him deeper into his chair.

'Frog Shefflin,' he said dully.

'And you?' probed Mother Sutton.

Ware nodded, putting an arm about the setter and pulling the animal close to him. The move was significant, the gesture of a man trying to put dark and grisly shadows behind him, while clinging to something warm and true and substantial. There was a hint of loneliness of spirit there.

Mother Sutton went at her bread mixing a trifle fiercely. 'Alive,' she said tersely, 'Hampton Rudd had his good points. Dead, I'm not so sure. He left too much on your shoulders, Logan. It is grinding the youth out of you, throwing ugliness and dangers at you which are not of your making. It will leave scars on you as long as you live.'

'A man must do his job,' said Ware somberly. 'The trouble was really Mize Huncutt's doing. He's been pushing Shefflin at me for some time.'

'That girl, Loren Rudd, she's in town, I hear,' said Midge.

Ware nodded. 'She was with me. Shefflin might have hit her. She's pretty badly upset. Can't blame her, I guess. She's not used to such things.'

'Is anyone?' demanded Mother Sutton. 'It's left a sickness in you. Midge, put on the coffeepot.'

The setter pushed closer to Ware, a moist tongue gentle across his hand. There was no further talk for the moment. These women possessed deep wisdom. They knew that it was not words which Logan Ware needed at the moment. It was just to sit quietly in this bright, savory kitchen while the soothing balm of normalcy of things spread across a raw wound to soothe and heal. They watched the bleak tide of feeling gradually lessen and ebb from him and the quieter, steadier things take hold. Under his shock of dark, tousled hair his face softened, grew more boyish, and they were thankful. By the time coffee was ready he had climbed out of the pit of bitterness.

There were golden-brown doughnuts to go with the coffee and as he bit into one Ware smiled at Mother Sutton. 'Another reason why I hope you'll come out to the ranch,' he said.

'Me?' Mother Sutton was startled. 'What do you mean, Logan?'

Ware said, 'To keep house for a while. I figure to persuade Loren Rudd to come out to

Hat headquarters. There will have to be another woman there, of course, with wisdom and understanding. You'd be perfect for the part, Mother Sutton. You remember once you said you'd like the chance to change that empty tomb of a ranch house into something livable? Well, here's that chance. And I'll put in the rest of my life blessing you.'

Mother Sutton stared at him. 'You really mean that, don't you?'

'I sure do. With Steve coming home tomorrow, Midge won't be alone. She can run this cottage.'

'If you can get Loren Rudd into that Hat ranch house, you'll be doing something her own father was never able to accomplish,' declared Mother Sutton.

'More reason for you to come. Make it easier for me to persuade her.' Ware took a small packet of currency from a pocket and laid it on the table. 'Two hundred dollars of honest Hat money. Proceeds of a sale of some Hat cows. Your month's wages.'

'Nonsense! If I come it won't be for money.'

'If you come it will be for money,' said Ware calmly. 'You'll earn it, just making doughnuts.'

He went over to a little crockery jar which stood on the end of a kitchen shelf. More than once he had seen Mother Sutton go to that jar when she needed some grocery money. He tucked the wad of currency into the jar and replaced the top.

'I'll be by for you in the morning with a spring wagon. Thanks for everything. You two people are good for a man's soul.' He picked up his hat and started for the door.

'And where are you going to sleep tonight?' demanded Mother Sutton.

Ware shrugged. 'Dub Pennymaker's got a good hayloft. Won't be the first time I've bunked there.'

'Not this night, you won't,' said Mother Sutton firmly. 'There's Steve's old bunk up in the attic. It's all made up. Go have you a good sleep, Logan Ware.'

The stairs to that little attic room were outside, climbing the back wall of the cottage. Speck, the setter, padded at Ware's heels and, when Ware turned in, settled down beside the bunk with a sigh.

For a time, weary as he was, Ware had trouble luring sleep. Before his closed eyes hard and bitter pictures flashed, of men and their violent ways, of their cupidity and scheming greed, of much treachery and of some faith. And finally of roaring guns winking redly in the night and of a man dying harshly with nothing to leave to the world except a railing at fate or at luck or at an inscrutable destiny.

These things jangled along Ware's nerve ends, but the stillness and security of this frugal cottage were at work. The tension ran out of him and when the relaxation of sleep stole over him his arm dropped down beside the bunk, his hand falling limply to rest on the setter's shoulder. The setter curled a furry head against it in warm content.

CHAPTER THREE

THINNING RANKS

Logan Ware waited outside the door of the Valley House. The morning of a new day lay cool and fresh along the street. The poplar leaves shimmered, dew-washed and clean. The violence of the night before was as if it had never happened, for the endless turn of time could not be held back because of the puny idiocies of men. Only the minds of men had leisure to reflect on things that were done with and, right or wrong, could not be recalled.

Stubby Hoffmeyer came out and murmured, 'She just went in, Logan.'

Ware nodded, tossed aside the cigarette he'd been breakfasting on up to this point, strode into the hotel dining room.

Loren Rudd was at a small side table. Other diners had been up and gone a full half hour before. The girl was pale and subdued-looking. Ware drew out a chair across from her. He said, 'This is pure business, ma'am. The talk we have to have. Consider me somebody you've never seen before.'

She looked at him from a grave and hostile distance. Ware had borrowed Steve Sutton's razor and, clean-shaven, the deep-tanned leanness of his face stood out in stark, bold lines. Sound sleep had cleared his eyes, freshened him all through. You could, thought the girl, like him or hate him, but you could not ignore him.

'There is,' she said curtly, 'nothing I wish to talk to you about, ever!'

'There is if you expect to claim any part of the inheritance your father left you,' Ware told her quietly. 'You'll be interested to know that there is a proviso, drawn up and signed at a later date, which must be complied with before the provisions of the original will are valid. That is what I want to explain to you.'

'Mr Bennett knows nothing about such a proviso,' she flared.

'There are,' drawled Ware dryly, 'several things Mr Bennett knows nothing about. The same goes for Mize Huncutt, Lister Beckwith, and Dobe Yarnell.'

'What are the terms of this—this proviso?'

'Why, before you can do as you wish with the Hat ranch, you must live there for a full year,' explained Ware. 'During that time I remain as foreman and have the last word of authority in all of Hat affairs. I hope you'll see fit to comply with it.'

The color of anger touched her face. 'That is

ridiculous. You—can produce this proviso?'

'When we get out to the ranch I'll let you read it with your own eyes,' said Ware.

'I've no intention of going out to Hat headquarters under such conditions,' she said stiffly. 'Let alone living there for a year.'

'You'll have to do it if you ever want to claim your inheritance,' Ware told her bluntly. 'Hat is a small empire, worth an awful lot of money. It represents something far too big and valuable to rate snap judgment. Whatever you finally decide to do with it, when it is fully yours, is your own business. But until that time I suggest you do this. Don't believe me, don't believe Tilton Bennett or Mize Huncutt or anybody else. Don't even believe yourself until you've had time to really understand what Hat can mean. The only way you can do that is come out there to live. Be sensible about this thing. Don't cut off your nose to spite your face.'

'I'm remembering last night,' she said flatly.

'So am I. But last night has nothing to do with your future. Despise me forever if you wish. That's your business. I'll keep out of your way as much as possible. You'll have companionship out at Hat. I've arranged for an older woman to come out and keep house for you.'

'But why should my father—Hampton Rudd—have drawn such a proviso to his will?' Her tone was not quite so positive as before.

'Suppose we let the future answer that,' Ware answered. 'Maybe it was because he was a very wise man.'

The waitress brought Ware's breakfast and he began to eat hungrily. He got satisfaction out of seeing that after some initial hesitation the girl did likewise. Presently she shot an abrupt question. 'If I refuse to comply with the provisions Hampton Rudd set up, what becomes of Hat ranch?'

'It becomes the joint property of the members of the Hat crew who helped Hamp Rudd build it up and maintain it. They can hold the ranch together on a partnership basis or liquidate it and share equally in the proceeds.'

'You are one of that crew?'

'Yes.'

'Then it would be to your personal advantage if I did not come out to the ranch to live. Why are you urging me to do so?'

Ware shrugged. 'Because I want to see Hamp Rudd's hope come true. Which is that you, his daughter, should own and possess and live on the ranch.'

'I don't understand,' cried the girl. 'It is all mixed up. You say that Hampton Rudd wanted me to have the ranch, yet in the same breath you tell me I can't have it unless I comply with certain silly provisions not written into the original will.'

'Not silly, but necessary,' corrected Ware.

'I won't do it! I won't go out there to live for a year. I have my own plans. I'll go to Tilton Bennett and have him set the machinery of the law to work. A will as stupid as that can and will be broken in court.'

Ware's eyes chilled. 'Hamp Rudd got no thanks and I've been told by several that I'll get none,' he said coldly. 'Which is probably right. But I'm doing this for Hamp Rudd, and nobody else. So it will be done the way he wanted it, or it won't be done at all. As far as Tilton Bennett and his kind of law is concerned, he's crooked as a drunken snake and he won't get to the start of the trail, let alone the end of it. If I have to get rough, I will. Long before Tilton Bennett and his law can even start breaking that will, there won't be enough of Hat left to worry about. You'll get nothing, which, it seems, is about what you deserve.'

The anger in her flared at him, but it bounced off the dark sternness of him with no effect at all. Uncertainty gripped her. This cowboy with the smoky gray eyes, the corded throat, and clean-cut jaw—there was a streak of granite in him. She had a feeling of helplessness.

'What proof have I that if I do as you ask you will live up to your part of the bargain and turn the ranch over to me fully?'

'The fact that I'm out to fulfill the final wish of your father,' said Ware. 'That's what he wanted, that's the way it will be.'

White teeth nibbled a red underlip. She shrugged. 'There seems to be nothing else I can do but comply.'

'Good!' Ware pushed back his chair. 'I'll be around for you in half an hour.'

She nodded, rising. Ware stepped aside, followed her out of the room. In the parlor Lister Beckwith was talking to Stubby Hoffmeyer. Beckwith turned swiftly, smiling, as the girl came in. 'Miss Rudd! I've been waiting for you. Tilton Bennett asked me to bring you over to his office. He has several ideas he wants to discuss with you.'

The girl hesitated and Ware drawled, 'Remember what I told you, ma'am. Don't believe Beckwith or Bennett or me or anybody else. See for yourself, first.'

'That,' said Stubby Hoffmeyer, 'is about the soundest advice I ever listened to, miss. What you see for yourself, you know for sure.'

Lister Beckwith turned on Stubby angrily. 'Any of your mix?'

'Mebbe,' shot back Stubby. 'This is my hotel. In it I think what I please and say what I please. Them who don't like it don't have to stick around. That takes in you, Lister.'

Loren Rudd said, 'There are developments I will talk over with you and Mr Bennett at a later date, Mr Beckwith. Right now I am going out to Hat headquarters.'

She turned away and went up the stairs.

Lister Beckwith stared after her angrily, then stamped out. Ware followed, grinning sardonically. 'When you tell one lie, Lister,' he drawled, 'why then you got to tell another one—quick! And after that some more, or the first two will get you by the throat and choke you. You just ain't thinkin' up plausible ones fast enough.'

Beckwith whirled, feet spread, a dark, hard hate in his eyes. 'You've been asking for it, Ware. You keep on asking and you'll be handed a chunk of hell that'll burn you alive. You got it in your head that people are afraid of you. That's a big mistake. You keep on tryin' to block the trail of justice and see where you end up.'

'When real justice comes along I'll take off my hat and step aside,' mocked Ware. 'But it's got to be the real thing, not the crooked brand you and Huncutt and Yarnell are tryin' to cook up. As for the hell—well, any time you feel that good, Lister—any time!'

Ware had spread his feet slightly and a blunt, thrusting challenge reached out from him.

'When I get ready to make my try,' Beckwith said evenly, 'I won't make the mistake Huncutt did. I won't send a stupid blunderer like Frog Shefflin.'

Beckwith moved away, cutting across the street to the Empire. Ware watched him out of sight, then headed for Dub Pennymaker's livery barn.

He got Dub's spring wagon and a team of broncos, tied his buckskin horse at lead behind the rig, then drove around to the Sutton cottage. Mother Sutton was ready and he put her in the rear seat, loaded in her frugal luggage, and drove to the hotel. Loren Rudd was waiting. Ware introduced her to Mother Sutton, stowed her luggage, and then, as the girl hesitated at the high step of the wagon, Ware caught her by both elbows and tossed her lightly up to the front seat. She colored sharply and stared straight ahead as Ware took his place beside her. The broncs hit their collars with a lunge and they went speeding down Lake Street.

From behind the half doors of the Empire, Lister Beckwith and Dave Grande watched the rig pass. Beckwith went into a flood of cursing. Dave Grande, in his cold, emotionless way, said, 'You don't whip a hombre like Logan Ware by cussin' at him, Beckwith. You don't whip him by sicking a fourth-rate gun fighter at him, like Huncutt did. Yonder rides a tough and able man. He won't fool easy, he won't whip easy, he won't kill easy. The man who pushes Ware off the driver's seat out at Hat will have to be smarter, tougher, and faster than he is. So far, I don't see anybody like that around.'

'You think you could do a better job than Mize or Dobe or me, maybe?' flared Beckwith. 'If so, demonstrate. There's rich pickings to be had.'

'So far I've left it to you others and seen nothing done,' said Grande curtly. 'Now I'm taking over myself. Things will begin to move.'

* * *

For a cow-country road, this wasn't a bad one. The team was full of run and the spring wagon spun briskly along. The tawny reaches of the valley ran away on either hand, with lingering mists still clotted like smoke in the hollows where the sun had not yet reached. North and east the bulk of Red Mountain lifted, blue with distance. The air smelled sweet and fresh and clean. There was just enough breeze moving to stipple the surface of Sunrise Lake with tiny, lipping waves.

Logan Ware pointed to the lake with his whip. 'Yours,' he told Loren Rudd. 'All of it. A mile wide and three miles long. The heart of your range. There are men who would cut a hundred throats to possess that lake and the grass which its moisture feeds on all sides. You were talkin' to four of them in Tilton Bennett's office last night.'

'What has been stolen, what has been pirated, must be returned,' the girl retorted. 'Else I'll never be able to live with my own conscience.'

'Then you'll part with nothing of your legacy,' Ware said. 'For nothing has been stolen, nothing pirated.'

'I don't care to argue,' said the girl crisply. 'The truth stands by itself.'

Ware did not press the point as he reined to a halt where the road swept closest to the lake's edge. Here, over a patch of tules and cattails, a cloud of ruby-winged blackbirds swooped and dipped, taking off with a rush of wings, then swinging about to light again until every tule tip bent and waved with the weight of one or more of the birds.

'Listen if you want to hear silver bells chiming,' Ware said.

The tinkling choral of the birds made a ceaseless melody. A white crane angled across the sky on slow, measured wingbeat, spotless against the morning blue.

Ware lifted higher in his seat, head swinging. Off around the curve of the lake shore sounded something else, a deep, hoarse, rumbling undertone. Out there quite a bunch of cattle were milling raggedly about some center attraction. Ware urged the team into motion, swung the rig off the road, and headed for the spot.

'What is it, Logan?' asked Mother Sutton.

'Bullfight. Old Thunder, our pure-bred whiteface, and a renegade mongrel that's drifted in. They were at it yesterday until Packy Maroon broke 'em up and headed Old Thunder down here to the lake. The renegade must have followed.'

Ware presently stopped the team, set the

brake, and handed the reins to Loren Rudd. 'I'll be back in a couple of minutes,' he said.

He went around to the buckskin, untied the lead rope, and swung into the saddle, riding at a lope into the milling cattle, scattering them as he closed in on the battlers. The fight had evidently been going on for some time. Over a considerable area the ground was gouged and furrowed by the driving, plunging hoofs of the bulls. The combatants were considerably the worse for wear, particularly the big, stocky whiteface.

The renegade was the same red roan Packy Maroon had told of, rangy, bony, and with wide-sweeping horns. It was the faster on its feet and those long, wicked horns had already got in some pretty savage work. Blood was dribbling down the sides of Old Thunder's neck and shoulders and long veils of slimy foam slavered from the whiteface's mouth.

Even as Ware watched, the renegade slipped away from one of the whiteface's heavy lunges, whirled, slashed, and barely missed driving a horn deep into Old Thunder's flank. The herd bull, heavy with weariness, just did swing clear.

This fight, Ware knew, could have but one ending if allowed to go on. In a test of pure strength the whiteface was easily superior. But the renegade was faster, shiftier, and had more endurance. Sooner or later it would sink one of those sweeping horns deep into the herd bull's vitals.

Ware spurred in close, trying to force the renegade away. But the red roan brute was wild with the fever of combat, its eyes wicked and rolling, its purpose in no way discouraged. It made a short, sharp charge at the buckskin, which danced nervously clear.

There was only one thing to do. Ware drew his gun, dropped it in line, and fired. The slug crashed accurately home and the renegade bull crumpled. Old Thunder stood there, flanks heaving in spasms of hard-won breath, a deep, growling bellow rumbling defiance.

Ware rode around the whiteface, looking it over carefully. There was a bad horn gouge in the off shoulder that could make trouble if the flies got into it. The dead renegade carried no brand.

Back at the wagon Ware tied the buckskin at lead again, swung, up to the seat, and took the reins from the girl. 'You killed one of them,' she accused. 'Now you leave it lay. Isn't that wasteful—and was it necessary?'

'I could have put in half a day chousing the renegade bull back a few miles,' Ware told her. 'But that wouldn't have done any good. It would soon have been back for more trouble. The renegade is worth the price of its hide, no more. But that pure-bred whiteface, well, it cost Hamp Rudd around fifteen hundred dollars by the time he got it out here on the range. Figure it out for yourself.'

'Who does the renegade, as you call it,

belong to?'

'Nobody. A maverick. Quite a few wild ones like it running loose back in the Butcherknife Roughs. And they stay there unless somebody makes a point to cut one out and head it down this way.'

'Why would they do that?'

Ware shrugged. 'Like I said, Old Thunder is a pretty valuable animal. The renegade would have killed the big fellow if I hadn't taken a hand. Some people wouldn't weep at seeing a prize Hat herd bull killed.'

'There must be an awful lot of people who hate Hat—with reason, no doubt.'

'We got our enemies,' Ware admitted dryly. 'Every big outfit has.'

The wagon rolled on up the long slopes and in time Hat headquarters came into view. The ranch house stood out from the other buildings because of its color. It was built of stone, a pale, tan native stone, hauled all the way from a certain rock face over at Shaggy Mountain. It was in the Spanish style, low and spreading, built around three sides of a stone-flagged patio.

A lot of time and money had gone into the building of the Hat ranch house. There were some who sneered and mocked and called it 'Rudd's Folly.' They knew the lonely hope which Hamp Rudd had put into the building and they scoffed, but never to his face.

It had a certain rugged beauty and the girl

gazed wide-eyed as Ware swung the spring wagon to a stop beside the patio entrance.

'It—it's amazing,' she stammered. 'I had no idea...'

'All the hope and all the loneliness in the world went into the building of that ranch house,' said Ware quietly. 'Hamp Rudd built it for you. I think if he could have lived to see you step across the threshold he would have died happy.'

The girl bit her lip and scrambled down from the wagon before Ware could get around to help her. Ware helped Mother Sutton down and the elder woman murmured, 'Give her time, Logan. She has much to unlearn.'

Ware carried the luggage across the patio, swung open the big, solid front door. 'It can stand a lot in the way of furnishings,' he said. 'Take your time and figure out what you'll need to make it comfortable. Make a list of things and I'll see that they are brought in. A year is a long time.'

When Ware got back to the wagon he found Tex Fortune standing at the heads of the team. 'The boys are waitin' in the bunkhouse, kid. Some things they want to know.'

Ware's eyes darkened. 'Mainly—who?'

'Morlan, Kelsey, and Trubee.'

Ware nodded. 'About as I expected. Things shake down.'

Quiet but potent tension lay in the bunkhouse. Rainy Day and Packy Maroon were there, too, Packy holding one end of a slim skein of horsehair, while Rainy braided it. In a way, this was significant. Whichever way Rainy went, that way would Packy go. And Ware felt pretty sure of Rainy. Ware looked the others over with blunt directness.

'What's on your minds?'

Ed Morlan spoke up. 'We want the whole picture. Where do we get off?'

'Meaning ...?'

'You've brought that girl out here. We know that she figgers to bust up Hat. That time comes, me an' Chain an' Buck want our share. We figger we got more right to it than such as Huncutt an' Beckwith an' Yarnell.'

'What makes you so sure Loren Rudd intends to bust up Hat?'

Morlan shrugged. 'There's talk. We been hearin' it for months, ever since Hamp Rudd died. We know why Hamp Rudd's wife left him, years ago. She might've thought she was right, but she had damn funny ideas. She insisted that Hamp Rudd turn back to Huncutt an' Yarnell an' old Draw Beckwith, Lister Beckwith's father, the range which they claimed an' which she figgered belonged to them. When Hamp wouldn't do it, she left him. That was before our time, but like I say there's been talk, an' we got that angle pretty clear.'

'Go ahead,' nodded Ware. 'What else?'

'All right. Hamp Rudd's daughter was born after his wife left him. His wife never would let him see the girl and she brought the girl up believin' that her father was a damned old range pirate, that he stole most of the range that goes to make up Hat. And she made the girl promise that if she ever got her hands on the ranch she was to turn back to Yarnell and Beckwith and Huncutt the parts they claimed Hamp took from them. Well, Hamp's gone an his wife's gone an' the girl's got the ranch. The talk is that she intends to do exactly what she promised her mother. That's right, ain't it?'

Ware nodded again. 'So what?'

'Why,' growled Chain Kelsey, 'if the girl's that anxious to throw away Hat, we aim to help her. We'll get our share. Like Ed says, we figger we got as much right, or more, to a chunk of Hat as Yarnell an' them others.'

'And how would you go about that?'

'Sell the cattle off an' split up the proceeds, for one thing,' said Kelsey bluntly. 'Make a real stake for once in our lives.'

'Turn cow thieves with a vengeance, eh?' drawled Ware. 'Be the same brand of coyotes as Yarnell and Beckwith and Huncutt—and Morry Seever and Spade Orcutt. No, thanks. You boys should have been more patient. Things you don't know. But it's just as well that I find out the real turn of your minds now. I might have been dependin' on you in a tight, later on, and been let down when it would really hurt. Get your stuff together. I'll go make out your time.'

He turned to Rainy Day and Packy Maroon. 'Those three just speakin' for themselves?'

'Just for themselves,' nodded Rainy.

Chain Kelsey, who had flushed hotly, said with a harsh snarling, 'Firin' Buck an' Ed an' me don't mean you're movin' us off the earth, Ware. We'll be around.'

'Your privilege,' Ware told him. 'One thing you want to get good and solid in your minds, though. A cow thief is a cow thief, even if he did ride for Hat at one time. He'll be treated as such.'

He turned to Rainy Day and Packy Maroon again. 'A chore for you boys. Take the spring wagon back to town. You'll need your broncs to get home on and to do this job down by the lake. That renegade bull you choused off yesterday, Packy—well, it followed Old Thunder down to the lake and they were mixing it when I came by with the ladies. Old Thunder is cut up pretty bad. I shot the renegade. You'll have to throw the whiteface down and put some balsam oil on his cuts to keep the flies away. If you want to skin the renegade for smokin' money, go to it. About all the brute is worth.'

There was a small corner room of the ranch house with an outside door which Hamp Rudd had used as an office. Logan Ware let himself in, got out his time and check books. A few minutes later he was out and over to the corrals again where Chain Kelsey, Ed Morlan, and

Buck Trubee were catching and saddling. Packy Maroon and Rainy Day were already driving off in the spring wagon, a pair of saddled broncs jogging behind.

Ware handed over the three time checks without a word. Chain Kelsey, dark-browed and saturnine, growled, 'If you think by getting rid of us you're goin' to grab all the gravy, you're wrong. You're due to learn a thing or two—the hard way.'

'Get gone and stay gone,' ordered Ware curtly.

He saw the flare sweep across Kelsey's eyes, rash and wild. For a moment he thought Kelsey might go for his gun and a rippling tautness went through him to meet the call. Then Tex Fortune's voice came across from the bunkhouse door, drawling but cold.

'Not today, Chain—for I'm lookin' right down your throat!'

Tex stood in an easy slouch, a Winchester rifle across his arm. Chain Kelsey cursed, stepped into his saddle, and spurred away. Ed Morlan and Buck Trubee, looking troubled and subdued, rode after him.

Ware walked slowly over to Tex. 'I'd liked to have kept Morlan and Trubee on,' he said. 'It's my feeling that Kelsey sold them somethin' they weren't likin' too well at the end. And you, well—thanks!'

Tex said, watching the departing riders, 'Any man's a fool to get to likin' another man overwell. If I had any sense I'd be feelin' like Kelsey does.' Then he grinned twistedly. 'Four of us left, kid—where they used to be nine. An' Hat range just as big as ever, with just as many cows on it. We got a chore ahead—a hell of a chore!'

CHAPTER FOUR

HOLDING THE TRAILS

For the next ten days Logan Ware and his remaining three riders virtually lived in the saddle, gone while the chill morning stars were still high and bright and coming back to headquarters on thoroughly fagged horses after night had claimed the valley. The four of them systematically rode the farthest limits of Hat range, drifting scattered cattle deeper toward the heart of Hat grass.

As Ware told the others, a lot of people were getting free and easy ideas toward Hat cows, now that Hamp Rudd was gone. The more the cattle were scattered, the more stragglers there were, the easier it would be for these people to drift out a few here, a few there. 'A big raid,' Ware said, 'we can trail down and do something about. But a dozen little raids would be too much for us, short-handed as we are.'

And so they rode and rode and grew lean and grim and weary. Ware and Tex Fortune rode a big circle away out past Red Mountain and spent three days out there, combing stragglers out of gulch and thicket. On their way home Ware and Tex stopped off at Guenoc to buy a good feed of oats for their jaded and ribby broncs and a square meal for themselves, since they had been living sketchily and frugally off what they could carry behind their saddles.

In the old days, before the railroad pushed a feeder line as far as Lockeford, over beyond Shaggy Mountain, Long Valley's only contact with the outside world had been by way of stage from Canyon to Harte City. In those days Guenoc had been an important way station along the stage road, thriving with business. Now stage travel between Harte City and Canyon had dropped to a single round trip a week and Guenoc had become pretty obscure. It still had a saloon and gambling hall where some of the wilder and more unsavory spirits of the valley liked to gather and hang out, and there was a hotel and eating house of sorts.

Logan Ware and Tex Fortune, shaggy, unshaven, and sun-blackened, cared for their broncs, then had the meal they were after. It was too late to start for home, so they decided to lay over for the night. To kill a little time before turning in, they went into the saloon and watched the game of draw poker going on there.

A couple of expressionless tinhorns were at the table, along with Black Tom Gaddy and a pair of saddle hands. Gaddy owned both the hotel and the saloon and his word was pretty much the law in Guenoc. One of the saddle hands was lank, hatchet-faced, pale-eyed. Neither Ware nor Tex had ever seen him before. The other cowboy was a sturdy youngster, hardly past voting age, curly-headed, open-faced. And, Ware soon decided, the lamb in the wolf den. For the other four were jockeying the kid, whipsawing him, and taking his money with almost contemptuous avarice.

Tex saw the way Ware's eyes were beginning to smoke up, so nudged his arm and murmured, 'I know it's raw, but still none of our pie. If that bald-faced kid learns his lesson the hard way, maybe it will do him good.'

Which was good logic, Ware knew, so he pushed his rising anger back and tried to feel indifferent. Then it became too raw, even for the curly-headed kid. One of the tinhorns, dealing, fumbled the cards slightly. The kid jerked straight in his chair and said, 'Wait a minute!'

A slow stiffening ran all around the table and a thin, strained silence fell. Then the dealer snapped, 'We're waitin'. What's bitin' you?'

The kid felt the hostility pouring his way, but he was game. 'I don't mind losin' to better cards in a clean deal,' he said. 'But it has to be clean.'

'Meanin'—what?' The tinhorn's voice was brittle.

'I've lost,' said the kid, 'on three kings. I've lost on three aces. I've lost on a high diamond flush, on queens full, an' even on four nines. The percentage don't run that way, unless things are framed. I had my suspicions. Now I know!'

Black Tom Gaddy swung his head and there was no mistaking the meaning of the glance he threw at each of the tinhorns and at the lank, hatchet-faced rider. The kid was way out on a limb and he didn't have a ghost of a show to get off it unless he backed down abjectly. Which, by the stubborn tilt to his jaw, he had no intention of doing.

'What do you know?' growled Black Tom Gaddy.

The kid tensed, going a little white around the mouth, for he knew what the next few bleak moments could mean. That was when Logan Ware said, 'Why, he knows the game is crooked, Gaddy. The same as you know it and I do.'

To which Tex added swiftly, 'Let's keep the discussion in the open. Which means—all hands on the top of the table. I said—all hands!'

It was one thing for Gaddy and these others to bull the kid into a corner, to make him crawl or take a chance where he had no possible vestige of such. It was something else to ignore these two Hat riders.

Black Tom Gaddy spread a pair of grimy, thick-fingered paws on the table, an example the others followed. Gaddy's glance was wicked as he turned it on Ware and Tex.

'All hell hates a meddler,' he snarled.

'And all creation hates a case game and them who run it,' Ware retorted. 'How much are they into you, friend?' he asked of the kid.

'Right around a hundred and fifty,' admitted the young rider.

'That's a lot of money to pay to find out you've been a fool.'

The youngster flushed, but admitted, 'I've been a fool, all right.'

'Get out of it while you still got your clothes and your skin. Write the rest off to experience.'

The kid managed a wry grin and Ware liked that. The kid said, 'With pleasure. And—thanks!'

He pocketed what money was left in front of him, pushed back from the table, and stood up. He looked around the table. 'I got a fair memory,' he said. 'Mebbe someday I'll meet you hombres where you're not ganged up an' where the bets will have to be clean. Then we'll see!'

He turned to Logan Ware and Tex Fortune. 'I got enough left to buy you gents a drink. I'd like to.'

'Better postpone that,' Ware said dryly. 'I think a little jag of ridin' will be good for all three of us. Doubt I'd enjoy my night's sleep around here.'

Tex gave a mock groan. 'Another night on the ground!' Then he grinned. 'One thing about the ground, there'll be no graybacks crawlin' around.'

They went out, Tex moving sideways so he could watch the four at the poker table.

Five minutes later, jogging out across the night with the murky lights of Guenoc fading behind them, Ware asked, 'Where, in particular, friend?'

'With my stake shot to pieces, anywhere there's a ridin' job, I reckon,' answered the kid. 'An' make it Russell—Curly Russell.'

'Ware here. Logan Ware. And Tex Fortune. How about forty and found, more hard work than you've ever met up with before, and a fifty-fifty chance of gettin' a hole shot in you within the next six months?'

'Sounds interestin',' said Curly Russell. 'No offense meant of course—but I'd like to know. Everythin' on the square?'

Ware liked this too. 'On the square. You'll be ridin' for the Hat outfit.'

Curly Russell whistled softly. 'You're right about that even chance of pickin' up a slug.'

Ware said, 'You're new to this country, else you'd never have sat into one of Gaddy's pet sheep-shearin' games. But you know things about Hat. I'm wonderin'—how?'

'It's like this,' said Curly Russell. 'I'm on the drift. I hit a little town up north called Aspen. I stop in at a store for some smokin'. A stage had just pulled in with some mail. A fellow comes in that I knew I'd seen somewhere before, yet I couldn't quite place him until he gave his name, askin' if there's any mail for him. Then I had him placed. The name was Maidlie—Slide Maidlie.'

'Ah!' said Tex softly. 'Tall jigger. Carries himself very straight. Beaked nose an' eyes cold enough to freeze a polar bear.'

'Right!' exclaimed Curly Russell. 'You know him?'

'Know of him. Keep talkin'.'

'Where I'd seen him before was at Larson Junction,' went on Curly. 'I was there with a shippin' herd one time. There was a shoot-out, Maidlie against two other guys. They buried the other two. Well, there's a letter at Aspen for Maidlie. He reads it, then starts askin' the storekeeper about the Hat outfit in Long Valley, how far it was from Aspen to Long Valley—things like that. It's pretty plain that Maidlie is figgerin' to head for these parts. So if, like you say, things are shapin' up rough and Slide Maidlie is goin' to be around, then somebody sure will stop a slug. It could be me. Or will Maidlie be ridin' on our side?'

'Not that I know of,' answered Ware. 'And I'm in a position to know. Guess you won't be interested in that job now?'

'You heard me say "our side," didn't you?' reproved Curly Russell quietly. 'I'm satisfied if you are.'

'It's a deal,' said Ware. 'Startin' now.'

Tex Fortune drawled, 'Frog Shefflin wasn't good enough, Logan. So now it's Slide Maidlie. That'll cost somebody money. But Maidlie is wicked enough with a gun to earn every cent of it. I met him once, back before I ever started ridin' for Hat. But this I know, he won't pull a Shefflin trick from the dark. When Maidlie calls a man it's a fair shake, out in the open an' face to face. Just the same, our troubles ain't gettin' any less, boy.'

'We'll meet 'em, one by one, an' not worry too much about 'em,' said Ware.

They bedded down in the open about ten miles from Guenoc and were up and riding again in the first gray light of dawn, breakfasting on cigarettes. It was mid-morning by the time they came in sight of Hat headquarters and, when they swung to a stop beside the corrals, two other riders came loping up along the town trail. One of these was Loren Rudd, the other Lister Beckwith.

Tex murmured, 'Enemy in camp. I'd enjoy puttin' a knot in that jigger's tail. Say the word, Logan.'

Ware shook his head. 'Let me handle this. Make yourself at home, Curly.'

Curly and Tex headed for the bunkhouse.

Ware turned to watch the girl and Lister Beckwith. He was startled at the change in Loren Rudd. The action of the ride had put blooming color in her face. Her hair had fallen loose across her shoulders and was pale copper in the sunlight. The severity was gone from about her mouth. Her eyes were shining with sheer exuberance of living.

Ware's face gave no index to his thoughts. His expression was inscrutable, hard-lined with weariness under the dust grime of travel and the dark shadow of unshaven beard along his jaw.

The girl sobered slightly under the intentness of his glance. She said, with just a hint of defense in her manner, 'Lister invited me to go for a ride along the lake shore. It was glorious.'

Ware nodded. 'That's fine. The more you see of your ranch the better you'll like it. Want me to take care of your bronc?'

'If you please.' She stepped lightly from the saddle, thanked Beckwith, and went over to the ranch house.

Ware swung his glance to Beckwith, who stirred uneasily in his saddle. 'Any reason,' he blurted, 'why Miss Rudd and I shouldn't be friends?'

'Depends,' said Ware briefly. 'Her friends are her affair. But—don't abuse the hospitality of Hat, Beckwith.'

'What do you mean?'

Ware shrugged. 'You know damn well what

I mean. If you're Loren Rudd's friend, you won't be party to any scheme calculated to rob her blind. So far, you have been. Maybe you've changed your mind. I wouldn't know about that, but I do know that you'll be judged by the company you keep, from here on out. It better be the right kind.'

'You don't trust many people, do you Ware?'

'I wouldn't trust you as far as I can spit,' said Ware bluntly. 'I thought I made that clear to you before.'

An angry flush burned across Lister Beckwith's face. 'You got a rough tongue.'

Ware's smile was bleak. 'I'm a rough guy in a rough world travelin' a rough trail. I never was worth a damn at being mealymouthed. I know where I stand and I like to know where everybody else stands. Particularly guys like you, Lister.'

'Time,' retorted Beckwith, 'will probably give you that answer.'

He swung his horse and rode away.

An hour later Logan Ware sat at the desk of the ranch office. He had shaved, had a bath and a change of clothes. He was entering Curly Russell's name in the time book when there was a knock at the inner door and Loren Rudd came in. 'You promised,' she said, 'to show me a certain document.'

Ware nodded and went over to the small, old-fashioned safe in one corner of the room.

He brought back the provisional conditions governing Hamp Rudd's will and, while the girl read them, went on at his work. At the rustle of the paper as she laid it down, Ware lifted his head and looked at her.

'Convinced?' he asked quietly.

She nodded reluctantly. 'It would seem that my father did not trust my judgment very far.'

'Was that his fault? You never gave him a chance to know you. It was the one thing he wanted above everything else. He clung to that hope up to the very hour of his death.'

The girl stared at the wall, her face somber. Ware asked, 'Does it shape up as so much of a hardship, having to spend the next year living here at Hat?'

'No,' she admitted. 'Not now. It isn't at all like I thought it would be. Everyone is—very nice to me. Even that fierce-looking little cook, Smoky Atwater.'

Ware grinned. 'If you pass muster with Smoky, that's the final test.'

She looked at him with measuring gravity. 'You are a strange person. I remember that—that night in town. And I see you as you are now. You could be two different people. It is a fact hard to get used to.'

'Put it like this,' said Ware. 'This is the way I would like to be—always. That night in Canyon was the way I have to be—sometimes.'

'You've been away a great deal since you brought me here. Once or twice I've awakened in the very early morning to hear hoofs pounding away. Then late at night there would be a light in the bunkhouse for a brief time. Do you and the crew always work that hard?'

'We work according to the needs of the ranch. It is a very big one, you know. I wonder if you realize how big?' He gave her rough dimensions measured in miles and a tally of cattle that ran into thousands. 'You are,' he ended, 'a very wealthy person. Have you and Mother Sutton decided on what the house needs to make it more livable?'

'Yes. We made up a list. I have it here.'

Ware glanced over it and the girl said dubiously, 'It will cost quite a bit of money. We can cut it down if you think there is too much.'

Ware shook his head, smiling again. 'It's not too much. I told you that you were a wealthy person. Hamp Rudd would have urged you to get twice as much. According to Hamp, money was made to buy the good things of life with. Only, Hamp missed out pretty much on the good things.'

'Why do you keep throwing that in my face all the time?' Her lips worked slightly. 'As though it was my fault...!'

'I guess,' said Ware quietly, 'I've been pretty bitter on that angle. About these furnishings, you'll probably like to pick them out yourself. I'll have one of the boys drive you over to Lockeford in the buckboard. Whatever you select I'll have Steve Sutton freight in for you.

You'll need some money.'

Ware got a checkbook from the safe, wrote, and handed the check to her. It was in four figures. 'You'll find they'll honor that at the Lockeford Mercantile Bank without question,' he said.

Loren Rudd took the check, glanced at it, and caught her breath. 'For so much? I won't know what to do with it all.'

'Spend it. It's yours. Buy everything you need. If you want more, holler.'

'My father certainly put great trust in you,' said Loren Rudd slowly. 'Maybe Smoky Atwater is right.'

She turned and hurried out, leaving Ware to ponder the strangeness of this last remark.

*   *   *

It was dark and chill. The stars were bright. The first hint of sunrise was still hours away. The buckboard was ready and Tex Fortune was grumbling.

'Why in hell pick on me? Why don't you send Rainy or Packy Maroon, or mebbe that new boy, Curly Russell? They'd plumb enjoy a ride like this with a pretty girl. What can I talk about to keep her interested. Why don't you go yourself?'

Logan Ware grinned. 'Do you good. Knock some of the onery crust off you. Seriously, there's two reasons why you're goin'. First, we could use half a dozen more riding hands, and I want you to try and round some up while Loren Rudd is at her shopping. Second, I want a tough guy with a gun ridin' with Miss Rudd when she's that far from home, for there's no tellin' what kind of ideas are brewing in the crooked skulls of certain people.'

Tex grunted, then growled, 'While I'm gone, don't you forget there's a gent named Slide Maidlie who's driftin' into Long Valley, and for a reason.'

'I'm not forgetting anything,' said Ware.

A slim figure came down from the ranch house, hurrying through the dark. Ware went to meet her. She gave an excited little laugh. 'It seems like the middle of the night. I had a dreadful time waking up. It's all like an adventure.'

Ware helped her into the buckboard, tucked blankets around her against the chill. Tex was silent, dour. Ware said wickedly, 'He's an onery old fossil—scared to death of a pretty girl. But he'll thaw out when the sun comes up.'

'I'll show the lady the time of her life,' growled Tex.

'Hold on a second,' said a voice from the dark.

It was Smoky Atwater, lugging a box from the cookshack. He put it in the back of the rig. 'A little grub I fixed up for you, ma'am,' he explained. 'Them miles can be plenty long an' make it quite a jump between meals.'

'Why, thank you, Smoky,' said the girl brightly. 'This is thoughtful of you. You are all—very kind.'

Tex kicked off the brake and the team, dancing with eagerness, surged away. The rattle of wheels faded.

'There rides one jim-dandy fine girl, Logan,' said Smoky. 'She ain't a bit like I was skeered she'd be. She's jest as friendly as an old boot. She come into my cookshack the other day, sat right down an' ate some of my raisin pie an' thought it was swell. Durned if it ain't mighty fine to have her around. Sorta puts a sparkle to the old ranch.'

'Yeah,' admitted Ware. 'But we don't want to forget that she came here with the idea of breaking up Hat and giving most of it away. So far as I know, she hasn't changed her mind on that. By the way, have you been discussing me with her?'

'Huh!' snorted Smoky. 'Where'd you git that idee?'

'This and that. Have you?'

'Mebbe,' admitted Smoky cautiously. 'She asks me a straight out question, I gotta answer her, don't I? An' you wouldn't have me lie to her, would you?'

Ware grinned in the dark. 'No. That's what I'm afraid of. You get started sometimes, you don't know when to stop. What did you tell her?'

'I didn't tell her you were a hoss thief, if

that's what's worryin' you,' Smoky growled. 'Anyhow, what I said is jest between her an' me an' none of your business.'

Smoky turned and stamped away. Ware laughed softly to himself.

Ware had breakfast with Mother Sutton. 'What do you think of her?' he asked.

'A lovely youngster,' said Mother Sutton simply. 'Trying to figure out a problem that is pretty weighty for so young a head. Brought up to believe that her father was an old pirate. What an injustice!'

'You think we can change her mind for her?'

Mother Sutton looked thoughtful. 'I'm not sure. I hope so. When she lets go she just bubbles with the sheer joy of living. Then she seems to remember something and she'll go quiet and get that set, severe look about her mouth. I could very easily hate the mother responsible for that, and I'm not the hating sort.'

Ware set Rainy Day and Packy Maroon and Curly Russell to another day of line riding, then caught and saddled and headed for town. Things had been quiet, these past several days. Too quiet. Ware was restless with the feeling that big things were brewing against the welfare of Hat.

Mize Huncutt and Dobe Yarnell were not through. They had, in fact, not yet begun. These were men whom Hamp Rudd, while alive, had held at arm's length and gun muzzle down through all the embattled years. Now Hamp was gone, but the material things he had held beyond the reach of Huncutt and Yarnell were still there. To think that these two would in any way lessen their efforts of conquest would be the sheerest folly.

There was also, mused Ware, something else to think about. Slide Maidlie.

Ware rode into Canyon at a slow jog. Dub Pennymaker was sitting, hunched on a stool, in front of his livery barn. The frayed and ancient straw hat which Dub wore, winter and summer, was pulled low over his eyes. But this could not hide the fact that Dub's face was a swollen, bruised, purple-and-black caricature of the human countenance.

Logan Ware reined in, stared, dismounted, and walked over to Dub, letting his horse sidle on of its own accord to the watering trough just around the shady side of the stable.

Dub looked up at Ware's approach. Dub's left eye was swollen completely shut, his right one was bloodshot and barely open enough for him to see.

'Good Lord, Dub—what happened to you?' exclaimed Ware.

Dub's thin shoulders lifted and fell in a slight shrug. Dub was a mild little man, with the years beginning to leave their mark on him. 'Fred Harmon,' he mumbled, through lips swollen and cut.

'Fred Harmon! Why, he'd make two of you.

When and why, Dub?'

'Last evenin'. The rest don't matter. I'm comin' along. I'm waitin' until I can see better. Then I'll settle for him.'

Ware built a cigarette, his hands shaking a trifle from the anger beginning to burn in him. The gray of his eyes went smoky. Ordinarily Dub Pennymaker wouldn't hurt a fly. Ordinarily he was cheerful, friendly, obliging. Out in the corral behind the stable were several old, worn-out, broken-down horses worth nothing to anyone for any purpose whatever. But Dub left them there and fed them and made shy excuses to those who scoffed at this unusual charity. Once, when completely cornered, Dub had awkwardly explained that when he got old and useless he hoped there'd be a friendly corral and a feed of hay a day for him.

As Logan Ware saw it, there was no conceivable excuse for anyone under any conditions to ever give a man like Dub Pennymaker a physical beating.

'You been to see Doc Abbey?' asked Ware.

Dub shrugged again. 'I'm comin' along. Just lemme sit here in the sun. I'm doin' all right.'

Dub's hands hung down between his knees, one clasped around the other, tight. Which didn't do any good, for, despite Dub's attempt to hold his hands still, they were trembling.

Ware said bluntly, 'You're not all right. You're a sick man. I'm going after Doc Abbey.'

'If Doc comes, he'll put me between blankets, Logan,' mumbled Dub in protest. 'An' I got chores to do around this stable with broncs to be fed an' took care of.'

'You darned, game, decent little rooster!' growled Ware. 'Quit worryin'. Those things will be taken care of too.'

Doc Abbey was a big, loose-framed, craggy-featured man. When he saw Dub Pennymaker's face he began to swear. He kept on swearing in a fierce, explosive way when he and Logan Ware got Dub laid out on the bunk in the harness and saddle room of the stable, and stripped the faded shirt from Dub's thin and ribby torso. Bruises as big as a man's spread hand splotched Dub's body.

Raged Doc, 'I'd like to have the whelp responsible for this on my operating table. I'd cut his heart out and choke him with it!'

CHAPTER FIVE

THE STRANGE WAY OF MEN

A warm, fly-buzzing gloom filled Dub Pennymaker's stable. Logan Ware toiled with hayfork, scraper, and scoop shovel. He filled mangers, cleaned stalls and pushed Dub Pennymaker's old wheelbarrow back and forth, dumping refuse on the pile out back of the stable. By twos, he led horses out and around to the watering trough to drink. At this chore he came finally to a roomy box stall, opened the gate of it, and went in.

A clean-limbed, copper-red filly crowded the far wall, trembling, and with wild rolling eye.

'Easy, Cherry—easy!' soothed Ware.

The behavior of the filly surprised him. He knew this horse well. The apple of Dub Pennymaker's eye, it was. The one horse in Dub's stable which he would neither loan nor rent to anyone. It was Dub's greatest pleasure to cinch a light racing pad on the filly and take it out for an exercise run. After which would come hours of brushing and rubbing down. The pretty animal was a pet and always before, when Ware had been in the stable, would have an eager head over the side of the stall, whickering softly for attention.

When Ware got close enough to lay a hand on the filly's shoulder, Cherry seemed to cower. Ware kept up a soothing murmur as he petted the animal. Then the gentle sweep of his hand ran across the animal's flank, stopped there, the filly flinching.

The usually sleek flank was rough, welted, feverish. A dry crust of something was there and a cloud of flies buzzed about Ware's disturbing hand.

Ware put a halter on the filly, led the nervous animal out to where the light was better. He swore with a cold, black anger. The filly had been as savagely spurred as any horse he had ever seen. Both flanks were torn and gouged, smeared with dried blood. In addition there were slanting welts where a quirt had been used mercilessly.

Ware tied the animal to a wall ring and went up to the harness room. Doc Abbey was just leaving.

'I got the poor little devil quieted down,' said Doc. 'Gave him something to make him sleep. Dub's a sick man, sick inside over something that's hurting him worse than the physical beating he took. I tried to get him to talk, but he wouldn't give me a hint. I'd like to know who did that to him.'

'Fred Harmon,' said Ware.

'Fred Harmon!' Doc exploded. 'It would be somebody like that damned hulking, pea-brained gorilla. But why should he have done this to Dub?'

'I think I know, Doc,' said Ware. 'Come here. As for Harmon—he'll be taken care of.'

Doc did some more swearing when he saw the little filly. Then he and Ware got to work. The mangled flanks were gently washed and cleansed, then smeared with a cooling, healing ointment. 'That,' said Doc, 'will do the job, in addition to keeping the flies away.'

As Doc spoke, hoofs sounded at the wide, main door of the stable. A big, rangy line-backed dun horse was there, its rider just dismounting. The rider came into the stable, leading the dun.

Logan Ware marked two things. The easy, confident way in which the dun paced at its master's shoulder, and the appearance of that master. A tall man, very erect. Low on his right leg, the butt flaring wide above the open-topped holster, a big black gun.

The stranger said, 'Want to board my bronc for a spell. The best the stable affords.' His tone was deep, decisive, crisp.

'Sure,' said Ware. 'Four bits a day.'

'Fair enough. Here's ten days in advance.' The stranger handed over a five-dollar bill, turning slightly as he did so. Ware glimpsed against the slanting light a profile that was beaked—fierce as a bird of prey.

Words which Curly Russell had spoken clicked in Logan Ware's brain. And he knew that here before him stood Slide Maidlie, gunman extraordinary!

Slide Maidlie! Who was being brought into Long Valley by somebody's money for one express purpose. To kill him—Logan Ware!

Ware went still and wordless, and he was startled when the gunman swore harshly. Slide Maidlie was staring at the sorrel filly's flank.

'Who did that?' he demanded. 'What low-down whelp would spur and mistreat a pretty little bronc that way? Any man who would do that to a good horse ought to be whipped half to death!'

Doc Abbey, who knew nothing of Slide Maidlie, his reputation or dread purpose in Long Valley, answered. 'A certain local character with instincts not a jump above those of something swinging by its tail to a jungle tree. I'm not a fighting man and don't care to be. But I'm liable to have me a damn good try at it if I meet up with this individual before I've had time to cool off.'

Doc snapped shut his satchel and marched off, bristling. Ware said to Slide Maidlie, 'Leave the dun here. I'll take care of it as soon as I've finished with the filly.'

Ware led the filly back to its stall. The pretty animal had ceased its shivering, its wild-eyed terror. The gentle ministrations of Ware and Doc Abbey seemed to have restored its confidence in mankind. When Ware took off the halter the filly lipped his sleeve, let out a long sigh, moved up to the manger, and began to feed.

Slide Maidlie was gone when Ware returned. The dun horse stood quietly and Ware unsaddled it, put it in an empty stall, brought it a measure of oats, and filled the manger with hay. Then he went to the harness room and looked in.

Whatever Doc Abbey had given Dub Pennymaker to make him sleep, it had not yet taken effect. At the slight creak of the door, Dub rolled his head and mumbled, 'Come in, Logan.'

Ware stood over the bunk and said, 'I just took care of Cherry, Dub. Doc and I fixed up those torn flanks. In a week Cherry will be as good as ever. That's what this is all about, isn't it?'

Dub nodded. 'Harmon's been tryin' to trade me out of Cherry for a long time. Yesterday afternoon I drop over to the Empire for a beer. Harmon's there, some likkered up. He starts the same old argument. I tell him again there's nothin' doin', that Cherry ain't for sale or trade or rent. He gets kinda rough with his talk, swearin' that someday he'll ride that bronc. I get a little warm under the collar and tell him that, knowin' the way he manhandles any bronc he's up on, I'd shoot Cherry with my own hand before I'd see him put a saddle on her. Then I had my beer and went to supper. I come back to the stable and set about my evenin' chores. I get around to Cherry's stall an' Cherry ain't there.'

Drowsiness was inching up on Dub. He blinked his one good eye and shook his head.

'Yeah,' he went on. 'Cherry's gone. I can't figger it. I think mebbe she'd nosed the latch loose on the stall door and wandered out. But she ain't nowhere around. Then, just at dusk, here she comes into the stable, with Harmon ridin'. He steps off, laughin' rough, sayin' he's made good his brag to ride my pet bronc. He said he wasn't interested in no trade any more, that Cherry wasn't bronc enough for him. I see the shape Cherry's in an' I guess I go a little crazy. Anyhow, I go after him. I didn't have much chance—much chance...'

Dub's voice trailed off. Ware said quietly, 'I get the picture, Dub. Now forget it and go to sleep. Cherry ain't hurt permanent.'

Dub didn't seem to hear him, but droned thickly on. 'Harmon gives me what for all right. When I'm down he puts the boots to me. He was like a mad dog, plumb enjoyin' himself. Pretty soon I go plumb out. When I come to, it's night. I ain't worth much. I manage to get the saddle off Cherry an' her into the box stall. Then I go out again. Come mornin' I'm straightened out a little. I make it outside, figgerin' if I sit in the sun awhile I'll get enough back so I can go tend Cherry. That's when you come along. Thanks, Logan—thanks...'

Dub couldn't say any more. Doc Abbey's sleeping potion finally got control. Dub began to snore.

Ware stopped in at Jake Farwell's store. As an excuse he bought a couple of sacks of smoking. Casually he asked, 'Seen Fred Harmon around, Jake?'

Jake shook a bald and bony head. 'Not today. He was in town yesterday, him and Milo Kron. What you interested in a pair of Flat Y hands for? They ain't ridin' on your side, Ware.'

'I know,' Ware said. 'But sometimes it pays to know more about them ridin' against you than with you. Anyway—thanks.'

Ware went out, stood in the shade of the poplars while he broke open a fresh sack of tobacco and built a smoke. His thoughts were running along two trails at once. Fred Harmon and—Slide Maidlie!

Harmon was of little consequence, just one of Dobe Yarnell's saddle hands who, because of the pure brute in him, had thrust an incident across the trail which set the cold fires of anger burning in Ware. But Maidlie ...!

The gunman was part of the main problem, a deadly actuality. Something had to be done about Slide Maidlie—and quick! But what? The obvious answer was to get Maidlie across the sights of a gun and finish him—for good!

But that was a setup from which Ware knew a normal shrinking. It wasn't exactly fear, though Logan Ware was young and he had no wish to die. Life was sweet, despite the growing weight of responsibility on his shoulders and the ever-towering cloud of inevitable conflict ahead of him.

Ware had never fancied himself as a gun fighter, nor had he any wish to be one. He carried a gun, as all men did in Long Valley. On occasion he used it, when he had to. Like against Frog Shefflin and that 'breed, Ute Rhyde. In each case they had started it. Maybe it was luck as well as fast, straight shooting that had brought him through. Luck, as Frog Shefflin had said, riding on his shoulder.

Maybe he was better with a gun than he knew. Maybe he was good enough to shade Slide Maidlie in an even-break showdown. If he wasn't, why then it would all be over swiftly, and the trust which Hamp Rudd had placed in him would be thrown away.

He looked at the sky, swept with sunshine, and wondered about a man's destiny. A man set out to blaze a trail and follow it. But life threw this and that at him until the trail was so cluttered it was hardly visible any more and was heaped high with mockery and strange frustrations.

Ware shook his head. Thoughts like these got a man nowhere. Regardless of the why and how of everything, a man had to act when confronted by problems which only action could solve.

He threw aside the butt of his cigarette and stalked off downstreet. A measured coldness seeped through him. You couldn't postpone some things, not with profit. There were challenges you couldn't dodge, regardless of outcome. Slide Maidlie was such a challenge.

Ware had the feeling that he would find Maidlie in the Empire, which he did. The gunman was at the bar, listening impassively while Dave Grande talked. A cold flicker shone for a second in Dave Grande's black eyes at sight of Ware. He set another glass on the bar and pushed a bottle up beside it.

'On the house, Ware,' he said. 'Have one.'

Ware nodded. 'Thanks.'

Dave Grande said, 'Shake hands with Slide Maidlie. Slide, this is Logan Ware.' There was a faint touch of emphasis to Ware's name.

Ware felt the impact of the gunman's blizzard-chilled glance, felt it running all up and down him, as though Maidlie was examining him in the minutest detail. Then he nodded and put out his hand. His handshake was firm, strong. He said, 'Glad to meet you, Ware. How's the little filly?'

Ware tipped the bottle, barely covering the bottom of his glass. 'All right. Be good as new in a week. That dun of yours is a nice bronc. Whickered like an eager pup when I poured it some grain.'

Maidlie chuckled. 'Cougar's a damn big baby. But I like him so. Sorry I took you for the stable roustabout. No offense. Where was the feller who owned the stable?'

'Laid out on a bunk in the harness room, all beat to hell. The same whelp who worked out on the filly worked out on him. I just took over to help out a friend.'

'Guess I'm not up on the latest news,' put in Dave Grande. 'You mean Dub Pennymaker ran foul of some trouble?'

'Put it that he ran foul of a damn lousy coyote,' answered Ware.

Hoofs rattled to a stop out front. Then spur chains clashed and two riders came in, the leader swinging the half doors with a heavy-handed push. Ware, his glass halfway to his lips, put it down untasted and came well around.

Sight of Fred Harmon brought back all of the cold, furious anger Ware had known when he first beheld the wreck of Dub Pennymaker's face and heard who was responsible. And he remembered the cowering, fear-stricken little filly with the savagely torn flanks. He forgot all about Slide Maidlie. He hardly realized how his gun got in the hand he stabbed toward Harmon's thick body.

'You can stop right there, Harmon!' he rapped. 'Right there! Unbuckle your gun belt and let it drop. I mean—now!'

The room went very still. Harmon's thick lower lip sagged in startled bewilderment. He ran his tongue across it and blurted, 'You loco, Ware? What's pinchin' you, anyhow?'

'I'm thinking of Dub Pennymaker, all beat to hell. A man two thirds your size and damn near twice your age, Harmon. Then I'm thinking about that little Cherry bronc, Dub's pride and joy, all ripped and spurred and bloody.'

'You mean, Ware,' came Slide Maidlie's voice, 'that there stands the hombre who cut that filly's flanks to pieces?'

'There he stands,' nodded Ware. 'Sweet specimen, eh? You heard me, Harmon! Unbuckle your gun belt and get rid of it. Then I take mine off and you and me step out into the street!'

'This,' said Slide Maidlie, 'I'm going to enjoy.' His voice went frosty. 'You with the crooked jaw—if you got any ideas of siding your pug-ugly friend—don't!'

Milo Kron took one look at Maidlie's eyes and then said, his words sliding gutturally across his twisted jaw, 'I'm not packin' any torch.'

Fred Harmon seemed to have finally got the import of things through a bullethead and he wasn't at all averse to the prospect. He had a lot of confidence in the weight of his fists and in his rough-and-tumble ability. He jerked loose his belt and let it and the gun drop on a chair. He backed through the half doors and Ware followed, laying his gun on a poker table as he passed.

The moment Ware emerged, Harmon made his rush, both fists clubbing. One missed, as Ware ducked. The other bounced off the side of Ware's head, knocking his hat off, staggering him.

Ware ducked lower, dove in close, driving a shoulder into the pit of Harmon's stomach, almost lifting him off his feet as he bulled him back against the hitch rail, which caught Harmon just at the hips, making him waver wildly, momentarily off balance. That was when Ware stepped back and hit him.

The full store of Ware's banked-up anger went into that punch. It drove Harmon's head back, pulped his heavy lips, bringing a gush of blood. Ware hit him twice more, a left and a right, the last another solid, lifting smash. Harmon went backward over the hitch rail, legs waving wildly. He landed flat on his back in the dust of the street. But there was a lot of animal vitality in Fred Harmon's thick body and he recovered swiftly, getting up on one knee as Ware ducked under the rail to follow up his advantage.

This was a careless move on Ware's part, for it brought his unprotected face within Harmon's reach. Harmon swung a punch while still on his knee.

The blow crashed home under Ware's left eye and he felt like he'd been kicked by a horse. It dropped him to his hands and knees and Harmon, reaching out a clawing hand, caught Ware by the shoulder and dragged him close, bringing in another short, chopping blow to Ware's face. Then he threw his weight on Ware, driving him back and down.

A numbness froze Ware all through and his head was dazed and thick. Instinct alone made him push both hands up, grab Harmon's jaw on either side with hard-gripping fingers, and push his head back. The bulk of Ware's rigid arms shielded his own face and jaw in large part and Harmon's mauling blows for the moment were wild and not too damaging.

The respite was short, but it was enough to let Ware's head clear somewhat and lessen the numbness that clogged his muscles. Harmon left off trying to pound a fist home, instead grabbing at Ware's wrists in an effort to drag that clamping grip off his face. Ware put all his strength into a sideways push and it threw Harmon off him. Ware rolled the other way, lurched to his feet.

Regaining his feet did things for Ware. The panic of desperation he had known when Harmon had him down left him. A certain brittle, calculating coolness of thought came back to him. His head snapped clear, strength flowed back into his legs, and when Harmon came at him, raging furiously over the advantage he had lost, Ware side-stepped the rush, followed it, and caught Harmon as he turned.

Harmon was spinning into the punch and Ware leaned everything he had behind it. He aimed for the angle of Harmon's jaw, just under the ear, and found the target fairly. The punch hurt Harmon badly, shook him up, made him flounder. Ware followed in and sent him reeling wildly with another smash to the same spot.

Ware never lost this advantage. He followed his man mercilessly, hitting like a machine. There was no tautness, no pinch to his muscles, now. His shoulders were loose and he snapped his punches in with wicked force.

But Harmon was tough, with that sodden toughness common to men with a brutish make-up. He was thick and solid and heavy. Though dazed and foggy and clumsy, he kept pawing back and there was still high danger in his blows.

Ware was oblivious to everything but the man in front of him. He did not see or hear Mize Huncutt and Dobe Yarnell as they came riding down the street with Morry Seever and Spade Orcutt. He did not see the hot light which sprang into their eyes, nor the significant glances they traded back and forth, nor the way they presently maneuvered their horses until they had formed a rough square about him and his opponent. He saw nothing but the bleeding, wobbling bulk of Fred Harmon in front of him and he kept on winging punches in a bitter, all-consuming purpose to batter Harmon down into the dust.

His fists and wrists felt numb from the battering shock of repeated impact. He thought he never would get this burly brute down. But there was a limit to what even Harmon could take. When he did break he caved all over. He did not fall violently, he just seemed to crumple and sink and then Ware no longer had a target for his aching, weary fists.

Ware's own legs were trembling. He spread his feet to steady himself, rocking back and forth. Breath ran in and out of him with a raw, salty rasping. He dragged a shirted arm across his face, wiping away some of the blood which smeared it. He blinked his eyes against the sting of sweat, stared down at Harmon. 'I reckon,' he mumbled, his battered lips clumsy, 'that Dub Pennymaker will rest a little easier now, Harmon.'

Ware turned away, toward the Empire. That was when Dobe Yarnell said, 'Just a minute, Ware! Where d'you think you're goin'?'

Ware blinked again, looked around. He saw Yarnell and Mize Huncutt, Morry Seever and Spade Orcutt. Seever had a plaster over his eye and his face was pinched and venomous.

Cold shock ran through Ware, wiping the thickness from his mind, clearing his eyes. Again he swung his glance, turning completely around, slowly. He saw the purpose in these four, saw it climbing higher and higher toward the explosion point. They had him dead to rights—had him cold!

He didn't even have a gun. But that, he knew, wouldn't stop them. Here, in one wicked moment, they could rub out the one big obstacle which stood in the path of their purpose against the Hat ranch. It wasn't egotism on Ware's part which made him realize that, with him dead, Hat resistance must inevitably crumble. And the way things were in Long Valley at the moment, Yarnell and Huncutt could bluster their way out of a cold-blooded killing.

Morry Seever and Spade Orcutt hated him venomously. It thrust out from them like some poison breath. They wanted him for purely personal reasons. And while Dobe Yarnell and Mize Huncutt also hated him, their main purpose was a material one. They had to get him out of the way to have free conquest of Hat.

They were no longer sure of their chance of success by preying on Loren Rudd's sincere but misguided theories concerning the ranch. She had moved out from under their thumbs, was living at Hat where her theories might change. So it was high time to strike by other means. This was one of them, a golden opportunity.

Ware could see all this going through their minds, saw the wicked decision forming. Something came up inside him, some white and deathless flame. His shoulders straightened, his head came up and from his battered lips burst his defiance.

'You damn yellow cowards!'

Behind Ware sounded a deep, cold voice. 'Good kid! That's tellin' them!'

The next moment Slide Maidlie stood beside Ware. Under the gunman's beaked nose his lips pulled thin with contempt. His eyes were at their iciest. 'Now then,' he taunted deliberately, 'what was it you were figuring on doin'? Maidlie's the name—Slide Maidlie!'

The look of consternation which leaped into the eyes of Dobe Yarnell and Mize Huncutt was almost ludicrous. Spade Orcutt grunted as though struck a blow. Morry Seever's hands, which had been shifting and flickering restlessly, grew still, crossed on the saddle horn.

A tight, sardonic smile touched Maidlie's lips. 'Ware was right,' he said scathingly. 'You damn yellow cowards!' He dropped a hand on Ware's shoulder and his words fell distinctly. 'Come on, friend. You need some wet towels on your face and a slug of liquor under your belt.'

After the fury of combat and the deadly threat that had momentarily stalked the street outside, it seemed cool and almost restful in the Empire. It was good to sag back in a chair and hold a wet, cold towel against a bruised mouth and face. For a time reaction held a man weak and heavy, but then the deep wells of a man's strength began replenishing and he could stir to activity again.

Logan Ware laid aside a final towel, buckled on his gun, brushed dust from his hat. He and Slide Maidlie and Dave Grande had the Empire to themselves. Dobe Yarnell and Mize Huncutt had not come into the place at all. They had set Milo Kron, Spade Orcutt, and Morry Seever to the task of boosting Fred Harmon into a saddle and then all of them rode out of town. They had to hold Harmon in his saddle.

Ware held out his hand to Slide Maidlie, looked at him steadily through swollen lids. 'Thanks, Maidlie,' he said. 'I'm not sure I didn't make a fool of myself. I sure got way out on a limb and it was cracking badly when you stepped in and got me off it. I owe you plenty for that.'

'You went out on that limb for a friend, didn't you?' Maidlie said, his handgrip firm. 'Well, that justified it. You don't owe me a thing. Good luck!'

Ware went out. Maidlie stared after him, cold eyes narrowed and inscrutable. Dave Grande said, 'You could have saved a lot of people a lot of trouble if you'd stayed out of the picture, Maidlie.'

The gunman looked at Grande and Grande flushed. 'A man like me,' said Maidlie coldly, 'makes few friends. But every now and then I run across a man I like. I like Logan Ware. I like the straight up-and-down, gutty make-up of him. The proposition you offered me? I'm not interested.'

Slide Maidlie tipped his hat over one eye and stalked out of the saloon, a tall man, very erect, hawk-faced and formidable.

Dave Grande stared at the doors until they had quit winnowing. Then he cursed and in his black eyes a hard red glint flickered.

CHAPTER SIX

DEVIOUS TRAILS

Behind a string of steadily plodding mules two big, new Merivale freight wagons, lead wagon and back action, turned into the lower end of Lake Street and rolled ponderously up to Jake Farwell's store. The yoke bells of the leaders of the team sent a clashing, cheerful cadence along the street. Up on the box Steve Sutton balanced, his raw-boned shoulders swaying easily to the lurch of the lead wagon, jerk line in one hand, brake strap in the other. As he swung the freight outfit to a creaking stop he called cheerfully, 'Hi, cowboy! Why all the heavy thought?'

Logan Ware looked up. 'Hello, Steve!'

Steve stared and exclaimed, 'Holy smoke! What have you been pushing your face against?'

Logan Ware shrugged. 'Did you pass Tex Fortune and Loren Rudd along the road?'

'Yeah,' said Steve, swinging down across a wheel. 'I wondered about that. The girl fed up with ranch life already and pulling out?'

Ware shook his head. 'Going out to Lockeford to order up a flock of furnishings for the ranch house. It'll be your chore to haul them in next trip.'

Steve Sutton spread his feet in front of Ware and said, 'You still haven't said what hit you. Man! Have you got a pair of shiners, along with various others signs of rugged conflict. If you got licked, don't be too proud to admit it.'

A bleak smile touched Ware's battered lips. 'I came close, too close for comfort. But I didn't get licked. When do you figure to make your next trip out?'

'First of the week. Why?'

'Then you'll be around for two or three days. You can do Dub Pennymaker's stable chores for him. By that time he'll be in shape again to handle things for himself.'

'What happened to Dub?' demanded Steve.

Ware told him and Steve swore softly. 'I'd like to have seen you giving Harmon a dose of his own medicine. That guy has been askin' for a good clubbin', far back as I can remember. You don't care how much misery you pile up for yourself, do you? He'll be layin' for you.'

'A lot of people are laying for me,' Ware said dryly. 'One more or less doesn't matter.'

'How's Mother doing out at Hat?'

'Enjoying herself, I think. Why don't you and Midge come out for a visit?'

'We will, one of these days,' promised Steve. 'How you making out with Huncutt and Yarnell and that crowd?'

'Quiet, just now.'

'Let's hope it stays that way. I'll be glad to look after Dub and his chores.'

Ware looked in on Dub when he went over to the stable after his horse. Dub was deep in sleep, yet even so he twitched and whimpered now and then, his battered nerves not fully quieted. Ware told himself he was glad he'd evened up for Dub.

He thought about it all as he rode out of town. In some ways it had been a fool play. Viewed in cold blood, it wasn't the smartest thing in the world to shoulder other people's troubles when he was already overloaded with his own. Yet there were times when anger piled up in a man to a point where cold-blooded judgment didn't mean a thing.

As far as Fred Harmon's undying enmity was concerned, he'd have had that anyway, for Harmon was one of Dobe Yarnell's pet bully boys. But in the fury of the fight he'd let Yarnell and Huncutt ride up and get him hopelessly cornered. Which wasn't so good. Neither was the fact that Morry Seever and Spade Orcutt, once of Hat, were now definitely riding with Huncutt and Yarnell. Well, coyotes ran with coyotes, by preference.

The biggest item of importance was the stand Slide Maidlie had taken. That *had* been a surprise, and a mighty welcome one. Right now, Ware realized, he owed his life to Slide Maidlie. The gunman who, by all reasonable logic, had been brought into Long Valley for the express purpose of making good where Frog Shefflin had failed had, when the chips were down, stepped in and sided him. He, Logan Ware, was alive right now because Maidlie had done this. It was something to make a man wonder about, for a fact.

Of course, it might have been just a whim of the moment, carried out by Maidlie for the purpose of heightening his bargaining power with Huncutt and Yarnell, making them dig deeper to get him and keep him on their side, a reasonable move on the part of a professional gun fighter whose lethal ability was for sale to the highest bidder.

There was no question but that Slide Maidlie was a cold and deadly proposition. Yet, thinking about him, Logan Ware had to admit to a strange liking for the man. In Maidlie's crisp, firm handshake and in the directness of his icy eyes was a certain self-respect and adherence to principle. None of the coarse, treacherous brute, like Frog Shefflin.

Whatever the purpose behind Maidlie's action, there was no telling. For that matter there never was any telling about a professional gun fighter.

Back at the ranch, Ware cleaned up the marks of conflict as best he could, then went over to the office for a few hours of good, solid work. Of late he'd not had too much chance to get all the ranch records up to date, what with the press of more active outside work.

Hamp Rudd had put great store in keeping a real written record of all of Hat affairs. It had been Hamp Rudd's contention that more than one ranch had gone on the rocks because of slovenly and careless bookkeeping. If a man did not keep proper records, so Hamp had claimed, then he didn't know just where he stood at all times. And if he didn't know where he stood, then he didn't know where he was going, and that put him in the class of a first-rate fool. There was more than one reason why Hamp Rudd had built Hat up into the outfit it was. Shrewd business sense wasn't the least of these.

Ware had been at the desk for a good two hours when through the open window at his elbow drifted the patter of hoofs and the skirl of buckboard wheels. Ware looked out to see none other than Tilton Bennett, the lawyer, head his buckboard team in against the corral fence, then heave his gross bulk ponderously to the ground. Ware went out and stood on the office doorstep. Bennett came over, a bland, almost jovial look on his heavy-jowled face.

'I was hoping to find you here, Logan, but afraid I wouldn't. Mind if I come in?'

Ware shrugged. 'Not at all.'

The lawyer sank into a chair, wheezing. He looked around and said, 'Hamp Rudd was a shrewd man. Never left anything to chance, did he?'

'He knew how to run a ranch,' said Ware briefly. 'What's on your mind?'

'Mainly a talk with you and Miss Rudd.'

'It will have to be with me alone. Miss Rudd is not here.'

'Not here! You mean—she's gone back to Harte City?'

'No, just to Lockeford. She should be back by tomorrow evening at the latest. But I'm listening.'

Tilton Bennett got out a black cheroot, lighted it, and mouthed it mostly. 'I thought you might be interested in knowing that I have decided not to represent Huncutt and Yarnell and Beckwith in their claims against Hat.' He cocked an eye appraisingly to measure the effect of these words on Logan Ware.

But Ware was poker-faced. 'Interesting. Why?'

'My position has been entirely professional. I do not hold with violence. I told Huncutt and Yarnell and Beckwith that when I first agreed to represent them. I exacted their promise to abide strictly by the due process of the law. Er—that promise was not kept. That Frog Shefflin affair the other night was proof of such. Therefore I feel that I am released of my commitments to Huncutt and the others.'

'I see,' said Ware. 'That is what you wanted Miss Rudd to know?'

'In part—in part.'

The lawyer puffed furiously at his cheroot and Ware waited, knowing that all this was merely an approach to the real object of Bennett's visit. Bennett seemed to be searching very carefully for words.

'I'm glad of this opportunity to speak to you alone,' the lawyer went on slowly. 'Er—Miss Rudd might not thoroughly understand. In refusing to represent Huncutt and Yarnell and Beckwith, I am forfeiting a very sizable retainer fee. I am not in business for my health. I am bidding for business. I feel that if I were retained by Hat interests in opposition to the claims of Huncutt and those others, then my services to Hat can be of very considerable value.'

Bennett took the cheroot from his wet lips and held it out in front of him, staring at it, giving the impression that he was waiting almost breathlessly for Ware's answer.

Ware's expression became even more inscrutable. 'That,' he agreed, 'could very well be.'

'Exactly!' exclaimed Bennett eagerly. 'I'm sure of it. In addition I now possess information very advantageous to Hat's cause.'

'I can see how you would have,' murmured Ware.

'Then it is a deal?'

Ware shrugged. 'I'll have to talk it over with Miss Rudd first and get her wishes in the matter. I'll let you know.'

'I have,' said Bennett sententiously, 'undergone a change of opinion on certain matters. After carefully considering the matter from all angles I am now of the opinion that it would be the worst of folly for Miss Rudd to part with any portion of her inheritance without full monetary consideration.'

'That,' said Ware crisply, 'has always been my opinion. Glad that we agree.'

Bennett beamed. 'I would not like to see Miss Rudd's true interests jeopardized. For she is a lovely girl.'

'Yeah,' nodded Ware. 'Lovely.'

Bennett heaved his bulk from the chair. 'I'm disappointed in not finding her here at the ranch. You will inform her of the purpose of my visit?'

'I'll tell her.'

Ware stood in the office door, watching Tilton Bennett drive away. Then he spat, as though to relieve his mouth of some foul taste.

* * *

Just at sundown of the following day Tex Fortune rolled the Hat buckboard to a stop at the corrals. Logan Ware went over to meet it. Loren Rudd scrambled down before Ware could offer an aiding hand. She was dusty and tired but happy-looking.

'Have a good spree?' Ware asked, smiling.

'A spending one,' exclaimed the girl. 'I'm afraid I've been horribly extravagant. But it is partly Tex's fault. He kept on encouraging me.'

'He would,' drawled Ware. 'He's an

irresponsible sort.'

Tex snorted. 'That so! Me, I know how to give a young lady a good time. We understand each other, Miss Loren and I do.'

The girl was staring at Ware's face, her expression sobering. 'There's been—trouble?'

'Not too much. I stopped a couple of fists. Got some news for you. Can I see you after supper?'

'Why—yes, of course. The trouble—what was it?'

'I took a swing at an hombre I didn't like. He swung back. That's all. I'm glad you had a good time.'

She hurried off to the ranch house and Tex, as he began unhitching the weary buckboard team, said, 'All right—whose fists did you stop—and why?'

Ware told him, briefly. Tex swore. 'You can be the damnedest fool! Borrowing more trouble when you're gettin' round-shouldered from the load you're packin' now.'

'If you'd have seen Dub Pennymaker and the way that pet filly had been mishandled, you'd have done the same,' Ware retorted. 'I met Slide Maidlie.'

'Ah! I hope you didn't spit in his eye.'

Ware told the rest of the story and Tex whistled in stark amazement. 'And Maidlie sided you? I will be damned! That could mean that Maidlie and whoever sent out for him couldn't come to terms.'

'Could be. We'll find out before long, I reckon. Have any luck picking up some new hands?'

'Just a couple. Brothers. Joe and Speck Larribee. I kinda liked the looks of them. They'll be in sometime tomorrow.'

'We can sure use them. Morry Seever and Spade Orcutt have gone over to Huncutt and that crowd. Chances are Chain Kelsey, Ed Morlan, and Buck Trubee will end up in the same corral.'

'Wouldn't surprise me,' growled Tex. 'If we could just get Slide Maidlie on our side! He'd be worth a dozen like Orcutt and Kelsey and such.'

'No chance,' said Ware. 'I wouldn't hire him on a straight gun-fighter deal. He'd have to chouse cows with the rest of us and I doubt he'd care for that.'

'Don't be so damned proud,' said Tex bluntly. 'If you can get him, do it on any deal he wants to name. Unless all signs fail, chousin' cows is goin' to be of minor importance in the near future, while fightin' for Hat an' our own skins is goin' to be the big chore. If you can get Maidlie, get him. Before he ties in on the other side an' gets you.'

After supper Ware took his cigarette out to the edge of the benchland on which headquarters stood, and looked down across the valley. The night had settled in, warm and still; the black void of the valley seemed steeped in peace. But Ware well knew what was brewing out there, the gathering forces of explosion. This thing could never be settled amicably. Tides were running out there, dark and devious ones, driven by the hates and greeds of men. Envy, trickery, double-dealing—and in back of it all the inevitable final judgment that would be written in gunsmoke.

A light step sounded behind him and Ware turned. It was Loren Rudd. Ware said, 'I was just about to come up to the office.'

'That's all right,' said the girl. 'We can talk here just as well. What is this news you said you had for me?'

Ware told her about Tilton Bennett's visit and what the lawyer had to offer. She was startled.

'I don't understand. Does that mean Mr Bennett does not believe the claims by Yarnell and the others against the ranch are legitimate?'

'He knows they're not, and never were,' answered Ware.

'Yet my mother—'

'I'm glad you mentioned her,' cut in Ware. 'There's no question about your mother being sincere in her beliefs. But she was wrong. You understand I mean no disrespect when I say that?'

'Yes. But surely she would never have felt as she did without good cause.'

'Individual viewpoint enters there,' countered Ware. 'She was born and raised in the East under sheltered conditions. She was on her way out to California by stage to visit relatives when she met Hamp Rudd, was swept off her feet by a whirlwind courtship, and married him. She never did come to fully understand this country and the men in it. Try and visualize Long Valley as it was in those days. A wild, tough wilderness, with great cattle possibilities, particularly for a ranch built around Sunrise Lake. Hamp Rudd, along with other men, saw and understood those possibilities. It was open range and the best of it would go to the man strong and tough enough to take it and hold it against all comers. Hamp Rudd was that man. He didn't pirate any range, he didn't steal it. He just met other men in open fight for it and whipped them. If he hadn't won, then someone else would have taken all of what makes up Hat today.'

'Mother did not see it that way,' argued the girl. 'She saw dark, brutal days—of fighting and dead men. She saw riders brought in across their saddles. More than once she saw my father come in smeared with his own blood. She said that life was one long nightmare to her and when she begged my father to change his ways he would not. So, she left him.'

'It was unfortunate that your mother simply could not come to understand the accepted rules of the fight your father put up to win his share of a raw and ruthless frontier.'

'Could she be blamed?'

'No. But she could have been mistaken. Hamp Rudd kept on building up Hat in the hope that she would one day realize that and come back to him, bringing you with her. That was the great hope of his life, for no other woman ever meant a thing to him. He was a product of his time, Hamp Rudd was. Unchanging in his hates, unswerving in his loyalties. Ruthless when he had to be but gentle in many strange ways. And never a thief, never a range pirate. Just a man who built and hung onto what he built. And a realist, a hardheaded realist.'

'But how could my mother have judged him so wrongly if things were like you say?'

'Because she just couldn't understand the rules of the West,' said Ware. 'Some of those rules have not changed. You met up with one of them that night in Canyon. Kill or be killed. It was Frog Shefflin—or me. You've come to understand that now, haven't you?'

She was silent for quite an interval. When she answered her voice was muffled. 'I think I have. About Mr Bennett, what made him change his mind?'

'Tilton Bennett,' said Ware bluntly, 'is a shyster, pure and simple. He was with Huncutt and the rest while he thought there was a chance to profit. When you came out here to

Hat to live the picture changed. Bennett figured he'd been betting on the wrong horse. So now he wants to get back on the other side of the fence and he's willing to trade secrets he had with Huncutt and that gang, to us for money. Bennett is crooked as a snake. I wouldn't trust him out of my sight.'

Again she was silent for a time. She laughed a little hesitantly. 'There seem to be several things I'll have to change my mind about. You must give me time.'

Ware looked down at her. The reflected light of the stars laid a thin highlight of silver along her profile and the faultless curve of her throat. Here was loveliness. A stir ran through Ware and he might have said many things had not, at that moment, the click of hoofs sounded, coming up the slope.

Ware listened a moment, then took the girl's arm and turned her toward the ranch house. 'Scatter along,' he said. 'Visitors coming.'

She stood her ground. 'Who is it?'

'Don't know. Which is why I want you safe inside.'

'No! I'm staying right here.'

There was no further time to argue, for the hoofs were close now. Ware stepped well apart from Loren Rudd before challenging the dark crisply. 'Who's ridin'?'

Bit chains jangled as horses were reined in. A drawling but alert voice asked, 'Is this the Hat ranch?'

'That's right.'

'This is Speck and Joe Larribee. Feller named Tex Fortune told us we'd find ridin' jobs here. We didn't expect to show up until tomorrow, but then we decided we might as well drift in early.'

'Fine! Light and make yourselves at home. I'm Logan Ware.'

'You're the man we were to report to. Looks like this might turn out to be excitin' country. Real interestin', in fact.'

'What do you mean?' asked Ware.

'Well, things were boilin' down in that town of Canyon when Speck an' me come through. Folks were considerable worked up over a killin' that had just taken place.'

'A killing?'

'Yeah. The guy who got it was one of these lawyer fellers. Bennett, I think the name was. Somebody took a potshot at him through the window of his office, while Bennett was sittin' at his desk. An' they didn't miss!'

CHAPTER SEVEN

RAID BY NIGHT

Joe and Speck Larribee were tall and lean, thin-faced and leathery. Logan Ware liked the looks of them as he sat across the table from them in the cookshack and watched them wolf the late meal Smoky Atwater had rustled up.

'I wouldn't try and misrepresent things,' Ware told them. 'What happened in Canyon this evening is just another grain of powder leading to the real blowup. Riding for Hat is going to be a rough trail.'

Joe Larribee shrugged. 'Your man, Tex Fortune, painted the same picture to Speck and me over in Lockeford. Which didn't worry us none, or we wouldn't be here. So long as the outfit we ride for is a clean one, Speck an' me will take our chances with the rest.'

'Mebbe,' suggested Speck Larribee, 'you got an answer as to why that lawyer hombre was rocked off?'

'Maybe. Put it down that an attempted double-cross has killed more men than one.'

'I see,' mumbled Speck through busy jaws. 'I see.'

When the Larribees finished eating, Ware took them over to the bunkhouse and introduced them to the rest of the crew. Then Ware went over to the office, got a lamp going, and set about entering the Larribees in the time book. The inner door opened and Loren Rudd came in. She looked pale and subdued and the severity was about her lips again. She spoke abruptly.

'Do you think Mr Bennett was killed because—because...?'

'Of course,' nodded Ware quietly. 'Because

he was all set to double-cross the crowd he'd been playing along with, and they knew it. They didn't want him peddling any secrets. They took the only way to be sure he didn't.'

The girl stared at nothing through clouded eyes. She said tautly, 'It's a terrible thing.'

'And just the start,' Ware told her grimly. 'From here on out anything can happen.'

'It hasn't changed,' said the girl, her tone bitter, 'this country hasn't changed. It's just like it was in Mother's day, cruel and ruthless and brutal. I'm trying to understand and see things as you want me to, but at times like this I hate it. I even wonder if I want any part of this ranch. It was built on savagery, blood, and brutality and it seems it will never change.'

'This is tonight,' Ware observed. 'Tomorrow, when the sun comes up, you'll feel different. Hat didn't kill Tilton Bennett. His own crooked greed killed him. Think of it that way.'

She glanced at him. 'This country's ruthlessness is in you too,' she charged. 'You are hard as stone. You are like Hamp Rudd must have been.'

'If I am,' said Ware, 'then I'm a lot of man. Now you run along and talk to Mother Sutton about all this. She'll make you feel better. I want to see laughter come back to your lips. It will be good for you, good for me, good for all of us. Yeah, tomorrow is another day. Always remember that.'

She stared at him a little somberly and he smiled. 'I think,' he said, 'we're coming to understand each other a little better.'

She did not answer, but as she turned to leave, Ware thought he saw a slight lifting of the shadow in her eyes.

Hours later, in the black dark of very early morning, Logan Ware stirred in his blankets and awoke. He heard Tex Fortune stirring also. He called, 'Tex! Hear it?'

'I hear it,' answered Tex. 'Down by the lake, sounds like.'

Ware pushed aside his blankets, padded on bare feet to the bunkhouse door, and listened. The sound was distant, but clear in his ears, now. The complaining bawl of cattle being chivvied in the dark. Tex was right. Something doing, down at the lake.

Ware dove back for his clothes and boots. He brought the bunkhouse fully awake with a harsh yell. 'Everybody up and out! Something wrong at the lake!'

They were soon at the corrals, catching and saddling in the dark. Horses were rearing and snorting, but the men worked with silent speed. Practiced hands, all, they soon were roaring down the valley slope. The night was a black mystery, the air rushing against their faces moist and chill. The horses, running full out, ate up distance.

Ware knew each pitch, each roll of the slope, its extent and direction. Unerringly he drove straight for the lake. Little groups of cattle, restless and stirring, scuttled out of the way of the straining horses. Ordinarily these cattle would be bedded quietly for the night. Not so now. Something had set them to moving uneasily.

In time, above the rattle of hoofs, the rush of air, the creak of gear, the moaning complaint of harried cattle lifted. It seemed to center mainly to the left and Ware swung that way, well to the east, coming in at the north side of the lake at a long angle. The forlorn moaning of the cattle deepened. Then, thin and shrill through the night, came a warning yell.

Out there ahead a gun winked red, report rumbling, and in the charging group Packy Maroon swore. 'My bronc's hit!'

Staggering and lurching, Packy's horse began dropping behind. Out ahead that gun winked again and a second joined it. Then Ware and Tex Fortune began shooting back. A taunting yell reached at them and a final flicker of gun flame. Then empty dark, with only that moaning, desperate bellowing of cattle left.

Ware charged ahead another couple of hundred yards, found nothing, so reined to a plunging halt, bringing the others to a stop with him. To the east, already faint with distance, speeding hoofs were fading into the night.

The others would have spurred after them, but Ware held to a halt. 'No use, boys—not in this dark. And they can't have cattle ahead of them, moving that fast. The deviltry they were up to is right here on the mud flat. I think I know what it is. Come on!'

They raced down to the lake shore, pulled up again there. Now their eyes were adjusting to the dark. Now they could make out the pale sheen of water, jeweled with star reflections. Out across the water loomed dark bulks, some looming high and large, others flat and smaller. Some of these bulks stirred and floundered, others lay still. Across the water came that moaning bellowing, with a strange note of despair and helplessness in it.

'Our drift fence,' gritted Ware harshly. 'They've cut it and stampeded a flock of cattle out into the mud. Some of them are down already. We got to move fast or we'll lose them. Two men stay on shore with the horses. The rest of us go out there. Tie riatas together, for we'll need the length. Rustle, everybody!'

Then Ware was out of his saddle and wading into the shallow water and the deep and treacherous mud beneath.

This was the only bad stretch of swamp along all of the lake's shore line. All else was firm enough to allow a cow or horse to wade out belly-deep with safety. But here an ancient adobe flat lay covered with water and had become seemingly bottomless mud. Any horse or cow that ventured out here was hopelessly bogged and doomed unless men came to its aid.

For this reason Hamp Rudd had, long before, built a stout barbed-wire fence, four strands high on deep and staunchly set posts, skirting this stretch of shore line, walling it off from venturing cattle. Now this fence had been cut and cattle driven through the openings into the treacherous mud. Some Hat cows would die this night.

'Tackle the down ones first!' yelled Ware. 'They'll drown if you don't!'

The lank figure of Joe Larribee came splashing and floundering up to Ware. Joe had hold of a riata end, dragging it over his shoulder. Together they seized the nearest down animal, dropped the riata loop over its horns. Then Joe yelled, 'All right, Speck! Set up on the pull!'

On the shore Speck Larribee threw a dally with the other end of the rope about his saddle horn, set his horse to taking up the slack, then, as the rope whipped taut, led his horse into a steady pull.

Out in the dark and the water and the mud, Logan Ware and Joe Larribee lifted and tugged at the bogged cow, yelling and urging. The cow began to struggle and the hold of the suckling mud gave grudgingly. The stout cow pony under Speck Larribee redoubled its efforts, hoofs chopping, haunches bunched and straining. The mud gave up the fight and the cow went slithering and skidding toward the shore.

Joe Larribee followed to bring back the rope. Ware singled out the next critter to be rescued. Over to one side Tex Fortune and Rainy Day were struggling with another animal, while on shore Curly Russell was setting his bronc to the pull. A yell of satisfaction by Tex signaled a victory there.

Ware thought, 'Two saved—but we'll never get them all out.'

They tried. They tried desperately. They labored without stop, without letup. They slipped and slid and floundered. They fell, got up, and fell again. They pulled and lifted until muscles strained to the breaking point. They were soaked with water and sweat. They were caked and smeared with mud. They fought on doggedly. Breath burned in their lungs, sobbed in their throats. No longer did they have breath to signal a victory pull. Their calls to the riders on the shore were mere croaks.

Long since had Packy Maroon, his horse dropping and dying back there in the dark, come panting up on foot, to plunge in unhesitating and bend his back to the killing toil. They got cows out of that death pit. Not all of them. Some they could not stir. Some were dead when they got to them, drowned when their heads sagged under the water. But they saved a dozen where they lost one.

The world was growing light with a new dawn as they got the last critter safely to dry land. One by one they staggered up out of the murderous mud, dropped in stupid weariness on solid earth to get some of the rest their tortured muscles cried for.

'All but seven, Logan,' mumbled Tex. 'We saved all but seven. That's my count.'

'All but seven,' Ware agreed. 'Better than I thought we'd do.'

Joe Larribee was scraping and rubbing his hands on the grass of the lake shore, trying to clean them of the worst of the mud and slime. Mixed with the mud and slime was the stain of blood, where a horn had gouged or a rope had burned. 'Lemme your smokin', Speck,' croaked Joe.

But Joe couldn't roll one, not with the mud and blood and cramped stiffness of his fingers. Speck quietly spun a smoke into shape for his brother.

Ware said, 'When I told you the trail would get rough, Joe, I didn't expect to throw a sample of it at you the first night in camp.'

Joe inhaled deeply. 'That's all right. Now Speck and me know the breed of coyote we're up against. Nothin' like learnin' that angle early. If a man's got it in for me, I say let him take out his grudge on me, personal. But not take it out on some poor damn dumb critter that can't fight back, just because it belongs to me. It takes a pretty damn low whelp to do that.'

'Somebody will have to stick around to

guard this cut fence,' said Packy Maroon. 'I'll do that while you fellers get back to headquarters and come down later with some more wire and tools. My horse is done for, anyhow.'

'You're not stayin',' put in Curly Russell. 'I am. You're soakin' wet, Packy. All I did was a little saddle work. You take my bronc home. I'll stick around here.'

As he spoke, Curly slid the rifle from the scabbard under his stirrup leather. 'Any more funny business with our cows and fence and somebody gets shot.'

Ware smiled wearily to himself. These three newcomers to the outfit, Curly and Joe and Speck Larribee, would definitely do. He thought, We'll be a damn tight little outfit, after all. Aloud he said, 'We'll be getting back. See you later, Curly.'

They climbed stiffly into their saddles, hunched shoulders against the chill of wet clothes and dawn air, and headed away up the long, swinging slope.

Curly stared after them. 'All my life,' he murmured, 'I been wantin' to tie in with an outfit that carried a real layer of salt under its hide an' that certain somethin' that spells class. Now I've found one an' here I stay.'

The approaching sun was piling up blinding light behind the gaunt bulk of Shaggy Mountain by the time Ware and his weary crew rode up to headquarters. They unsaddled, turned their horses into the corrals, then headed for the bunkhouse. Ware glanced up at the ranch house and saw Loren Rudd standing on the office step. She came toward him, so he went to meet her. He knew he was a mess, mud and slime from head to foot, and he smiled grimly at the question in her eyes.

'When I scour this off you'll be able to recognize me again,' he said.

'What on earth has happened?' she asked. 'It seemed like the middle of the night when I woke up, hearing some confusion and a wild racing away of hoofs. I knew something was wrong and I couldn't sleep another wink, worrying over you men. What was it?'

Ware told her, bluntly crisp. 'We got all the cattle out but about half a dozen—seven to be exact. And we lost one bronc. It's been a night that's cost Hat some money—and some sleep. Yet it could have been a great deal worse. If we'd been an hour later getting at the rescue job we'd have lost nearer fifty cows.'

As full understanding reached her, he was startled at the anger which flamed in Loren Rudd's eyes. 'What a cowardly, inhuman trick!' she cried. 'Deliberately driving poor dumb brutes out to die in the mud and water. What kind of men would do such a thing?'

'The kind we got hitting against us,' Ware said swiftly. 'Without principle, without conscience. Nice people—Mize Huncutt, Dobe Yarnell, and others. This night is something more for you to remember when you're trying to make up your mind about certain things.'

'None of our riders—were hurt?'

'No.' Ware hunched his shoulders against the clammy wetness of his shirt.

She was swiftly contrite. 'I'm sorry. I didn't mean to be selfish, keeping you standing there. Hurry and get some dry clothes on.'

He nodded. 'That's all right. I don't mind the wet, but this mud is something.'

She watched him stride off to the bunkhouse and she thought that some men would have looked ludicrous, in all that smear of mud. But Logan Ware just looked more the man, strong and sure and in balance. She went slowly back into the ranch house, thinking on this cattle empire her father had built, of the country he had built it in and of the men who peopled this country. Like men the world over, there were some who were devious and full of trickery. And there were some who were true...

She threw another look at Logan Ware, just as he entered the bunkhouse. Some who were true...

* * *

Over the breakfast table in the cookshack, Logan Ware told his men what lay ahead. They had cleaned up and were in dry clothes once more and wolfish with hunger.

'It's started,' Ware said bluntly. 'It was bound to come. They'll hit us here and hit us there. You boys will come closer to living in the saddle than ever before in your lives. We've got to patrol Hat range constantly. We'll sleep a little and eat when we can, but mostly we'll ride. As soon as I can locate some more reliable hands, I'll hire them on to help us. You'll ride with a short gun at your hip and a rifle under your stirrup leather. You'll shoot first and ask questions later. Whether Hat stands or falls will be decided in the next month or six weeks.'

They went out and caught up fresh broncs. Ware sent Joe and Speck Larribee out with Packy Maroon to look over the west boundary of Hat range. Tex and Rainy Day hooked up the buckboard, loaded on a spool of barbed wire, hammers, and staples, and headed for the lake. Ware caught up a bronc for Curly Russell and took it along at lead as he rode off after the buckboard.

They found Curly squatted on his heels, patiently guarding the cut fence. Ware said, 'I'll help you get the saddle off that dead bronc, Curly. Then you get back to headquarters and breakfast. After you eat you can ride a patrol out to the east.'

Curly nodded, picking up a blue denim coat jumper. 'Don't know which of the boys this belongs to, Logan. I found it yonder. I'll take it in with me.'

Ware stiffened slightly as his glance touched

the jumper. 'Let me see that.'

He took it, shook it out, and held it up. 'Tex—Rainy! Take a look at this. Ever see it before?'

'Yeah,' said Tex. 'Chain Kelsey used to wear it.'

'Right!' said Rainy. 'I was workin' over the same brandin' fire with him the day he got the scorch all across the back of it. A tough calf he was tryin' to wrastle down upset him into the edge of the fire. Where did it come from?'

'Curly found it laying over yonder.'

'Which means that Kelsey was here last night,' growled Tex. 'Lost it off his saddle mebbe, or laid it down while he was cuttin' our drift fence an', when we came ridin' in unexpected, rode off an' left it.'

Rainy swore softly. 'And once he rode for Hat. He's a bad one, Logan. He always was a bad one. I never did like him. Too damn secretive an' surly. Never opened up so you could get to really know him.'

Ware rolled the garment up, tied it behind his saddle. 'I'll hand it to him, next time I bump into him, and see what he has to say. Well, let's get at that fence.'

The wire-cutting job had been plenty thorough. It was past noon before they got the repair chore finished.

'Don't know how long it will stand,' said Tex. 'They may try it again.'

'We'll keep an eye on it,' said Ware. 'Just one

of a lot of things we'll have to keep an eye on.'

'We goin' to sit back an' let that damn crowd keep diggin' at us?' growled Tex. 'They'll nag us to death if we do. Me, I'm all in favor of packin' the fight to them, cornerin' them, an' then settlin' things, once an' for all.'

'That's just what they're hopin' we'll try,' Ware said. 'And should we try it we'd find them all set and waitin' for us—to cut us to shreds. They're goin' to dig an' nag at us, try and get us to lose our heads and go barging around high and wild until we ride into something. But the time ain't ripe for us to go after 'em that way. When it is, we'll move.'

Tex and Rainy loaded their tools back into the buckboard and were just about to head for headquarters when Tex said, 'Here comes that girl. She's a nice youngster an' a mighty pretty one, even if she has got some of her ideas kinda tangled. With things roughin' up across the range the way they are, she shouldn't be ridin' alone too much.'

Ware nodded. 'I'll speak to her about that.'

Loren Rudd waved to Tex and Rainy as they rolled past in the buckboard, then rode over to Logan Ware. 'I wanted to see the place of last night's trouble,' she explained. 'That nice, curly-headed rider of ours caught up and saddled a horse for me.'

She was, thought Ware, a stir running through him, as bright and lovely a thing as he had ever seen in a saddle, with the sun glinting in her hair and building warm tan across her cheeks.

'You shouldn't ride this far from headquarters alone,' he told her.

'Why not? I know the lay of the valley pretty well, now. I won't get lost.'

'It's not that, or the valley, either. It's just some of those who ride in it.'

She colored slightly. 'Really, I think you're trying to build up a threat that doesn't exist. Why should anyone bother me?'

Ware spun a cigarette into shape. 'I told you before that there are men who would cheerfully cut a hundred throats to possess this lake. I wouldn't say that if I didn't know it to be true. Well, you own the lake. You own Hat range and everything on it. With you as a hostage, the men who covet all you own would have an awfully strong trump card. Besides that, you are a woman—a lovely one. And in Long Valley, the same as any other place in the world, there are a certain number of two-legged brutes who only look like men. Believe me, I'm not talking just to make a noise.'

She looked at him, then away. 'I seem to be the cause of a great deal of trouble to you.'

'You are,' said Ware steadily, 'Hampton Rudd's daughter. All he built up and held together is yours. Hamp wanted it that way, wanted it more than any other thing in the world. He asked me to see that you got it. I'm just trying to fulfill his wish. So you see, there must be no harm come to you.'

She stared at the lake. 'You said there were seven cows you couldn't save. What's become of them?'

Ware pointed. 'Notice how the breeze is rippling the water? But right yonder there's a place where the ripple breaks and the water seems to rise and slide smoothly over something just beneath the surface? Well, there's the body of a cow at that spot. Over there's another and yonder still another. The mud is taking them down slowly. Soon it will have them entirely.'

The girl was very sober of face. 'I don't believe I ever really hated anyone in my life. Perhaps I never thought that far. But right now I think I hate the men responsible for such cruelty.'

'You're learning,' said Ware. 'I knew you would, once I got you out to Hat to live.'

'Let's ride,' said Loren Rudd abruptly, 'around to the place where the blackbirds sing.'

Ware stepped into his saddle and they set off at a leisurely jog. The girl sat her saddle lightly, all supple-muscled grace. Ware said, 'You deserve a better-lookin' horse than any which carry the Hat brand. There's one I know of I'd like to see you up on.'

'What's the matter with this one? It's a perfectly good horse.'

'Sure it is,' smiled Ware. 'But homely as sin. Just an ordinary, run-of-the-mill cow bronc.

Not decorative enough. It spoils the picture.'

'The picture,' said the girl severely, 'is this lake and the blue sky—this tawny valley and that shaggy blue mountain over there. Who cares for more?'

Ware did not answer, for he was staring intently out along the curve of the lake shore. Standing right up against a fringe of tules was a horse, saddled, but with saddle empty. A big, rangy, line-backed dun horse, standing quietly.

To the girl Ware said, his voice edged and sharp, 'Wait here!' Then, before she could answer, Ware spurred out ahead.

As he came up to it the dun lifted its head and whickered, a plaintive note of relief in the sound. Ware pulled in beside the animal, his glance running all around. Beyond the dun a thin line of tules had been pressed and broken down, as though something had crept through them or been dragged over them.

Ware swung down and moved past the dun, following that trail through the tules to the water's edge. There he found what he was looking for, sprawled on the mat of crushed tules.

Slide Maidlie, the gunman. Hatless and with all one side of his head smeared and matted with dried blood. It was not until Ware bent low over the motionless figure that he saw that Maidlie was still alive, still breathed.

CHAPTER EIGHT

LONG HATE

When Logan Ware emerged from the tules, carrying Slide Maidlie in his arms, Loren Rudd was there, white-faced and big of eye. 'Not—not dead?' she stammered.

'No. But like to be, from all appearances. Looks like the slug nearly scalped him.'

Ware put his burden down gently.

'Who—who is it?'

'Maidlie is his name. Slide Maidlie.'

Ware went back through the tules, scooped his hat full of water, and returned. Loren Rudd was out of her saddle and kneeling over the gunman, unknotting his neckerchief. 'Let me,' she said in a strangely quiet and determined voice.

She dipped the handkerchief in the water and began gently washing blood and dirt from that ragged bullet slash. Ware splashed the rest of the water on Maidlie's face and throat, then went back for more. He got back just as Maidlie stirred, groaned, and opened his eyes.

Maidlie mumbled unintelligibly, his voice thick and hoarse. Ware funneled the brim of his hat against Maidlie's lips and the gunman gulped desperately at the trickle of water. He closed his eyes for a moment, then opened them once more, and now the dull shock in them faded somewhat and they grew intelligent with returning strength. Particularly he stared at the girl bent over him, something almost like incredulity in the look.

'I guess it's real,' he mumbled. 'I guess it is. Some more—of that water?'

He drank again and then, when Loren Rudd rinsed out the neckerchief in the balance, Ware went back for still another hatful. This time, when he returned, Maidlie managed a grim, bitter smile.

'The wheels ain't goin' round and around quite so fast,' the gunman murmured. 'You're Ware, of course. The lady—could be an angel.'

'She's real, Maidlie,' said Ware. 'Can you remember what happened?'

'I'm ridin', taking a look at the country,' said Maidlie. 'I see the lake and cut toward it. Then my head explodes. When I come out of it, there's old Cougar standin' over me, whickerin' soft and anxious. I'm burning up with thirst. I remember there was a lake. I tried to get up and into the saddle but couldn't make it. All I can do is crawl, heading for the lake and water. I go out again. Next time I open my eyes it's night. I keep tryin' to locate that lake. I finally reach some tules and crawl into them. I go out once more. That's all I remember, until now.'

'Don't make him talk any more,' said the girl curtly. 'Loan me your neckerchief. I've got to manage a bandage of some sort. And some more water, please.'

Ware brought it and helped her with a crude bandage. 'If I get you in your saddle, do you think you can stick it for a few miles, Maidlie?' he asked.

'Tie me in and I'll have to stay put. Where away?'

'Hat headquarters. Hang onto yourself.'

Maidlie was reeling and wavering by the time Ware got him astride the dun. But after a moment the gunman steadied, straightened. 'I'll make it,' he said through gritted teeth.

With his riata Ware tied Maidlie's ankles to the cinch rings, brought the end of the rope up, and tied Maidlie's wrists to the saddle horn.

'There! You might sag a long way but you won't go completely off.' Ware turned to the girl. 'Take him straight home. If he goes out, don't stop. Keep right on traveling, for the quicker he's on a bunk, the better. If none of the boys are around, Smoky and Mother Sutton can help you. I'm going after Doc Abbey.'

The girl nodded, mounted, and took the dun horse's rein.

Maidlie turned his head painfully. 'In town, Ware—watch that fellow Grande. He's part snake, part wolf—and all against you.'

Ware watched them for a hundred yards or so, saw that all was going well, then climbed into his own saddle. He rode a short arc back from the lake edge, picked up the scuffed marks where Maidlie had dragged himself along, then backtracked. He found Maidlie's big black gun and retrieved it. Out nearly three hundred yards from the lake he found Maidlie's bullet-torn hat. Here was where the gunman had first fallen from his saddle. The only spot of cover that could have hidden the person who fired the shot was a small, isolated tule clump at the end of an outswinging arm of the lake. Ware rode over to it.

Sure enough, search showed a trampled spot in the tule cover. It also showed several cigarette butts and a single empty rifle shell which told nothing, as it was of a common and much-used caliber throughout the valley. The tule clump grew on a small hummock with the lake water lapping at the base of it. There, not fully erased by the action of the water, were hoofmarks, where a horse had stood.

The picture was clear enough for Ware. With his horse hidden by the elevation of the hummock and tule clump, someone had lain in wait and gulched Slide Maidlie as the gunman rode past. It was a happening for a man to think on soberly, as were Maidlie's parting words. Which was that Dave Grande was part snake and part wolf and would bear watching...

The warning against Grande hardly surprised Logan Ware. Thinking back on Grande, Ware saw him as a man behind a mask, secretive of thought and impulse, with black, cold eyes which no man could see or read. A man who held all other men at arm's length and who kept his own counsel in a remote and shadowy groove. Any sort of scheme might grow and take form in Dave Grande's guarded mind.

As for the attempted killing of Slide Maidlie, there could be any number of answers. Some old and unsuspected grudge by someone. The queerly twisted hunger which some men knew to bolster up their own lethal reputation by smoking down a known and feared gun fighter. Such hunters of doubtful glory seldom had the courage to make their try face to face with their victims, thought Ware.

In Canyon, Ware found Doc Abbey in his office, gave him the word about Slide Maidlie, then went down to Dub Pennymaker's stable to hook a team into a buckboard for Doc. Ware found Dub puttering about the premises, still plenty weak and shaky from his beating at the hands of Fred Harmon.

'What's the idea?' demanded Ware. 'Hasn't Steve Sutton been taking care of things for you?'

'Sure he has,' said Dub. 'Keeps all the heavy work cleaned up.'

'Then why don't you take it easy?'

'This ain't hurtin' me none. I wasn't made to lay around lazy.'

Doc Abbey came with his satchel and drove

away. Dub said, 'Folks sure are good to me. Steve Sutton doin' my chores. Doc takin' care of me and when I ask him how much I owe him he just says, "Ten years of friendship." Then you—I heard how you beat the everlastin' whey outa Harmon. I'm thankin' you for that, Logan. But you didn't have to do it. I'll get me even with Harmon, one of these days.'

A queer, bleak light came into Dub's faded eyes as he said this.

'You keep out of Harmon's way,' warned Ware. 'He's just a big dumb gorilla, but if he gets started on you again he'll break you in half. How's Cherry doin'?'

'Chipper. I been thinkin' about that little bronc, Logan. Don't seem right I should keep the filly corraled up so much. Cherry loves to run an' don't get near enough of it the way things are now. But the filly ain't cut out to be a ordinary cow bronc, ain't heavy enough or built right for it. If'n I knew somebody who'd use Cherry just for straight ridin' an' who'd treat her kind an' give her a good home, I'd make her a present to them.'

'That wouldn't be smart,' Ware said. 'Cherry's a valuable little bronc, worth considerable money.'

Dub shook his head. 'I'd never sell her. Was I to do that the money would never do me no good. I'd hate it an' hate myself. I could give her away, but never sell her. Guess that sounds kinda loco, but that's the way I feel about it.'

'I savvy how you feel,' admitted Ware. 'I'm sorry you won't sell her, though, for I was aiming to make you an offer for Cherry.'

'What did you aim to do with her if I would sell her?'

'Give her to Loren Rudd to ride. We got a lot of broncs out at Hat and they're all good cow broncs. But none of them got any real ridin' class to them. I'd kind of like Miss Rudd to have a real riding bronc.'

'You go put a halter on Cherry and take her out to Hat, Logan. Take her as a present from me to Hamp Rudd's daughter.'

'I couldn't do that, Dub. I'd buy the animal off you but not take her as a present.'

'You'll take Cherry as a present,' declared Dub stoutly. 'Why, Hamp Rudd's girl an' Cherry together would make a picture to gladden any man's eye. You take Cherry out to Hat with you or I'll do it myself. That's final!'

Dub was in deadly earnest about this and Ware knew he would hurt the old fellow deeply if he refused. 'I didn't come here to wangle your pet bronc as a present, Dub. You know that. But if this is the way you want it, all right. Hat will make it up to you in some way.'

'Hat don't owe me a cussed thing,' growled Dub. 'All the pay I want is that someday that girl ride by and let old Dub see how pretty her an' Cherry look together.'

'All right. I'll come by and pick up the bronc in a little while. But first, there's a few things I want to do around town.'

From the livery barn Logan Ware went up to the Empire. The place was empty except for Dave Grande behind the bar and Stubby Hoffmeyer, over from his hotel, having a beer.

Stubby waved Ware up. 'Have one with me, Logan. Hate to drink alone.'

Ware watched Grande pour the drink. 'What about Tilton Bennett, Stubby?' he asked quietly.

Stubby grunted. 'That's the question everybody is asking an' nobody seems to have an answer for. I heard the shot, but didn't think much about it. Then the news got around. Never was overfond of Til Bennett. He always struck me as bein' a little too quick to do most anything for a dollar or two. Still and all, that's a tough way to die, shot in the back by some sneakin' killer.'

'And nobody at all coming up with any kind of an answer as to who did it?' probed Ware.

'I ain't heard of any. One guess is as good as another, I reckon.'

'There's been a professional gun thrower hanging around town lately,' put in Dave Grande, his voice as cold and expressionless as his eyes. 'The breed that kill for money.'

'You're speakin' of that Slide Maidlie feller, of course,' said Stubby. 'Well—could be. Canyon sure is beginnin' to rough up. Sets a man to wonderin' what will happen next.'

'Maidlie didn't kill Bennett,' said Ware.

'He's not that sort. He's a gun fighter, yeah—but no cheap back-alley killer.'

'I see you go rustle out Doc Abbey,' said Stubby. 'Somebody hurt out at Hat, Logan?'

'Yeah. Slide Maidlie,' answered Ware, watching Dave Grande polish a glass. 'Somebody tried to gulch him, out along the lake shore. They held a little too high. Creased him. But Slide will make it all right.'

The glass slipped from Grande's fingers, crashed to fragments on the floor. Stubby Hoffmeyer, jumped, then grinned sheepishly. 'Doggone it, Dave—don't scare a man to death. With all this talk of sneak shootin' goin' on, any sudden noise like that gives me the fidgets.'

Grande reached for a broom. 'One time, just for the hell of it,' he said coolly, 'I tried to figure out the percentage of busting glasses behind a bar. The average was so long I got lost in ciphers.'

'Percentage,' drawled Ware, watching Grande with sardonic eyes, 'is something that's working all the time. For and against. A man never knows when it's going to hang his number on the board. Which is something slick schemers sometimes forget. Well, obliged for the drink, Stubby. Next time I buy.'

When Ware went out Stubby Hoffmeyer looked at Dave Grande with furrowed brow. 'That was a funny remark Logan just made. Wonder what he was drivin' at?'

Grande shrugged, his black eyes veiled. 'I wouldn't know. Didn't make sense to me.'

Stubby drained his glass, then observed, 'You can bet he meant somethin'. Logan's no fool.'

Back at the stable, Ware found Dub Pennymaker cinching a freshly cleaned and soaped saddle on Cherry, the sorrel filly. 'What's the idea?' he wanted to know.

'Saddle goes with the bronc,' said Dub. 'Now keep your shirt on. This hull never cost me a cent. A saddle drummer left it with me, years ago. He'd been haulin' it around with him tryin' to interest some of the womenfolks on ranches. You notice it's a smaller tree than usual. Anyhow, this drummer leaves it with me while he goes over to Guenoc. He sits into a game there and wins a lot of money. Next mornin' he's found by the trail with his head beat in. Ever since then the hull's been just layin' around my harness room, gatherin' dust. It's a right good little hull and should be just right for Hamp Rudd's girl.'

'You,' said Ware, 'ain't much to look at, Dub. But I bet was Doc Abbey to cut you open he'd find a nugget of pure gold where your heart is.'

Dub grinned twistedly. 'A chunk of rawhide, you mean.'

Logan Ware was cutting out past the lake on his way home, with Cherry trotting at lead beside his bronc, when, from the west, two riders came spurring. Ware went alert and inscrutable when he recognized Ed Morlan and Buck Trubee.

The two ex-Hat riders came up quietly. Ed Morlan said, 'You don't have to watch us like that, Logan. Buck and me been hopin' to see you. Wanted to say good-by and tell you we were sorry for being a pair of damn fools. You always treated us square, just like Hamp Rudd did, and we gave you a pretty raw deal by ridin' out on you the way we did. We must have been crazy. Anyhow, we're driftin' the country and we want to wish you good luck.'

'I didn't like to see you two leave,' admitted Ware. 'You always rated pretty well up in my book. One question I'd like to ask. Where were you last night?'

'Over at Pete Lord's cabin. Pete's some kind of forty-second cousin of Buck's, so we holed up with him. He sure told us what he thought of us for ridin' out on you.'

'He sure did,' mumbled Buck Trubee ruefully. 'But we had it comin'.'

There was no guile in these two. Ware could see they were telling the truth. He said, 'Why leave Long Valley? Why not come back and ride for Hat again?'

They stared at him. 'You don't mean—you'd trust us—after—after ...?' Ed Morlan stumbled to a stop.

'Why not? If you're interested, here's what I want you to do. Go to town and get a supply of grub and blankets from Jake Farwell. Tell him I said to charge it to Hat. Then line out for Red Mountain. Set up a camp for yourselves and then ride that country. I don't need to tell you what to do if you run across anybody tampering with our cattle. I'll drift up that way in a week or two and see how things are going. A deal?'

Ed Morlan drew a deep breath. 'You really mean that, Logan?'

'Sure I mean it. Your time starts again today.'

Morlan looked away and said gruffly, 'You're just plain square as hell. We don't deserve this. But you won't be sorry.'

Ware smiled. 'I know that, boys. Seen Kelsey around?'

'No!' growled Buck Trubee. 'And don't want to. After we left the other day he turned surly and gave Ed and me a nasty cussin' out because we didn't back his hand when he made the bluff of getting tough with you. We were already sick of the deal we'd let ourselves into and we got a good look at Kelsey then for the first time. So we split up. He went his way and we went ours. We ain't seen him since.'

Riding on toward the ranch, Logan Ware knew a grim satisfaction. Two more hands to bolster up Hat's thin force of riders. Ware knew he'd have no more trouble with Morlan and Trubee. They'd stick now, through thick and thin.

Arriving at headquarters, Ware found Doc Abbey just about ready to start back to town. Loren Rudd was talking with Doc. Ware asked, 'How's Maidlie?'

Doc said, 'Hard-skulled. In a week he'll be around, ready for more deviltry. What are you doing with Dub Pennymaker's pet bronc?'

Ware grinned. 'Taking it out for sunshine.'

Doc drove off. Loren Rudd said, 'That's the prettiest horse I've seen since I came to Long Valley.'

'Glad you like Cherry,' said Ware. 'Because she's yours.'

'Mine!'

'That's right. Present to you from Dub Pennymaker, along with the saddle.'

'Why—I don't understand.'

'Simple enough. Dub and me both agreed that you deserved to ride a prettier bronc than any this outfit can scrape up. So—Cherry is the answer.'

The girl stepped over to the filly, began petting the pretty animal. Cherry whickered softly, rubbed a velvet nose against the girl's shoulder.

'You see,' said Ware cheerfully. 'Cherry is a spoiled little brat. And will demand all of your time when you're anywhere near her.'

'She gorgeous,' murmured Loren Rudd, eyes shining. 'But I can't accept her, of course.'

'You got to. It's all settled.'

'Why,' asked the girl, looking at Ware

steadily, 'are you so good to me?'

'My chore, isn't it, to sell you on the idea that Hat is something for you to hold onto, just as your father left it to you? To do that I got to see that you have all the good things that Long Valley affords.'

'Doc Abbey told me where and how you got those bruises on your face.' The girl was running soft hands over Cherry's tender flank, now healing from the wicked spurring Fred Harmon had handed out. 'And this was the horse involved, of course. Doc said you were one of the few men he knew who would, as he put it, go all the way out on a limb for a friend. You seemed to be consistent at that. You've done it for my father and you did it for Dub Pennymaker—and because a horse was abused. There is a softness in you, Logan Ware. You are a strange man. I said it before and I say it again.'

Ware stirred, restlessly self-conscious. 'I make a fool of myself plumb regular,' he said, with an attempt at lightness. 'Dub said the only payment he wanted for Cherry was that you ride in on her and see him sometime. He said it would be a pretty picture, you and Cherry.'

* * *

Slide Maidlie was stretched on a bunk, a cap of clean white bandage on his head. He stretched out an eager hand for the big black gun Logan

Ware held toward him.

'It's been with me a long time,' the gunman said. 'Where'd you find it?'

Ware told him of the sign he'd worked out and how it read. Maidlie said, 'That hombre must have been well hid, for I never saw a thing. And I ain't the sort to ride around with my eyes shut.' He smiled grimly. 'A bad habit I got rid of early in life.'

'Any guesses as to who—and why?' asked Ware briefly.

'Maybe. The proposition they offered me just didn't suit, somehow. They could have been afraid I'd end up siding with you and Hat. So they decided to put a stop to that, quick.'

'The regular trail from town to the ranch here runs past the west end of the lake,' said Ware. 'So they sent somebody to watch it from a hide-out, in case you decided to head this way.'

'That seems to be the reasonable angle,' conceded Maidlie.

'You mention "they"?' reminded Ware.

'That fellow Grande, for one. He's the one who wrote me, got me down here. You watch him, Ware.'

'I will. Now I'll quit bothering you and let you get some sleep.'

'I don't want to wear out my welcome,' said Maidlie.

'When and if you do, I'll let you know,' Ware told him.

Ware went over to the cookshack and found Smoky Atwater elbow-deep in flour in his bread-mixing tub. Ware got together a snack for himself, cold beef and bread and cold coffee.

'Wedge of pie in the cooler,' grunted Smoky. So Ware got that too, and settled down at the table.

'Things are buildin' up, boy,' said Smoky. 'When they begin shootin' guys in the back, like Tilton Bennett got it, and when you start findin' 'em layin' by the trails, gulched, like that Maidlie feller, why, then the lid's off hell—complete.'

Ware nodded slowly. 'Their first scheming hasn't paid off. They tried the easier way first. Now they're beginning to get rough. We'll wait and watch. They'll have to make a big move pretty quick. We'll be there for the argument. One place we're making progress, Smoky. I think Loren Rudd is beginning to understand the true meaning of Hat, what's behind it and what it's worth.'

Smoky's eyes lighted up. 'That girl's the pure quill. When she got here with that Maidlie gent she called me out to help and, cool as you please, gave him a shoulder to lean on while we got him into the bunkhouse. She was right there handy while Doc Abbey was sewing up Maidlie's head an' slapping a bandage on it. She's no wilted vine, Loren Rudd ain't.'

Ware finished his frugal meal, spun a

cigarette into shape, and started to leave. In the doorway he paused, eyes narrowing. Up at the ranch house, standing beside his horse, was Lister Beckwith. He was talking to Loren Rudd. Beckwith had certainly come in quietly.

The girl darted into the ranch house but soon reappeared, pulling on a pair of small buckskin gauntlet gloves. Then she and Beckwith crossed over to the corrals. Ware walked to meet them.

'I've been wanting a chance to try out my new horse,' the girl said. 'Now I have it. Lister and I are going riding. Would you catch up Cherry for me?'

'Sure,' said Ware briefly. 'How are things, Beckwith?'

'Good enough.' There was a strangely guarded note about Beckwith. It was in his words, and in his eyes, far back, lay a light of something almost like uneasiness. He added, 'That Bennett affair was a nasty business.'

'Nobody seems to have the answer, there,' drawled Ware. 'You got any theories?'

Beckwith shook his head. 'I only know it was dirty business—and I don't like it.'

When Cherry was saddled, Ware handed the reins to the girl. 'Hop on, and I'll adjust the stirrup length of your new saddle.'

Beckwith said, 'I never imagined Dub Pennymaker would let go of his pet bronc. Cost you something, I'll bet that filly did.'

'Cost never figures between friends,' Ware

said enigmatically. 'That stirrup about right, Loren?'

It was the first time he had ever used her given name. He had spoken casually enough, but the girl darted a swift glance down at him. The brim of his hat hid all but the strong, brown line of his jaw. 'Yes,' she answered. 'That's fine.'

When they were ready to leave, Ware fixed direct eyes on Lister Beckwith. 'I said it once before but I'm reminding you of it again, Beckwith. A ride with Loren Rudd carries responsibility with it. And we think a lot of our boss on this ranch.'

Beckwith flushed and said, almost irritably, 'I'm no kid.'

Ware looked at the girl. 'Should you ever have cause, give Cherry her head. She'll run right away from anything in this valley.'

They rode off, the filly dancing with eagerness to run. When they were some distance out the girl turned in her saddle, looked back, and saw Ware still standing by the corrals, watching them. Impulsively she waved. Ware lifted a hand in answer. Then he went over to the office.

Hardly had he sat down at the desk than Mother Sutton came in. 'I don't like that, Logan,' she said bluntly.

'You mean, Loren going riding with Lister Beckwith?'

Mother Sutton nodded.

'What's wrong with it?' Ware asked.

'Several things. You're not forgetting, I hope, that Lister Beckwith was hand in glove with Yarnell and Huncutt in their first attempt to take advantage of that girl's mistaken ideas of what she should do with this ranch?'

'No. But it could be that Beckwith is undergoing a little change of heart regarding that.'

'Bosh!' exploded Mother Sutton. 'No Beckwith ever had a change of heart regarding anything where profit for a Beckwith was concerned. I knew old Draw Beckwith, Lister's father, and he was the most unscrupulous old scoundrel that ever lived. Lister is his father all over again, except in one thing. He hasn't his father's courage. But he certainly has all of Draw Beckwith's sly scheming, plus some of his own.'

'He can't do us any harm, taking Loren for a ride,' said Ware. 'There's been a big change in that girl. Hamp Rudd's blood is beginning to tell. The ranch is starting to get hold of her.'

'Men like you can be very stupid at times,' declared Mother Sutton. 'Consider this. Lister Beckwith is far from being an ugly, unattractive clod. To the contrary, he is a very handsome man. Nearly any girl, unless she happened to know his full background or notice that his eyes are a trifle too close together, could hardly help but be impressed by his attentions. Like so many with scoundrel blood in them, he can be very attractive and charming when he's of a mind to. Have you ever thought of that?'

'I still say he won't get far trying to persuade her back to her original intention of listening to any phony claims against Hat.'

'That's just the point. I don't think he'll try to. In my opinion Lister Beckwith is no longer scheming to get hold of part of the ranch. He's working to get all of it.'

'How?'

'By persuading Loren Rudd to fall in love with him, marry him. Those things happen, you know.'

Ware reached for his smoking. 'That's not being very flattering toward Loren, Mother Sutton,' he said slowly.

Mother Sutton dropped a fond hand on his shoulder. 'You have a streak of tough, uncompromising iron in you, boy. But deep down you're still an idealist. Should you ever fall in love it won't matter a bit whether the girl has a dime or a million. The girl herself will be the only consideration with you. All men haven't that honesty of heart. And while they might know some affection for the girl, the big thing with them is material gain. Such as getting a big, valuable ranch property along with the girl. In my opinion Lister Beckwith is exactly that sort of man.'

Ware smoked silently for a moment. 'What would you have me do—give Beckwith the run? I could do that, easy enough. But while I admit there's a lot about women I don't understand, it strikes me that the surest way to make Loren Rudd determined to go riding with Lister Beckwith would be to tell her she couldn't.'

'By that very remark,' said Mother Sutton dryly, 'you show you know a great deal more about women than you think. However, I still say that if there is any way you can discourage Loren from seeing too much of Lister Beckwith, you'd be wise to take it. For the man can be an attractive devil when he wants to, and who knows where a girl's heart may suddenly go? Sorry if I've given you something else to worry about, Logan—but I'm worried too.'

Ware reached up and patted Mother Sutton's hand. 'If,' he said quietly, 'Lister Beckwith tries any doublecross around here, he'll wish he'd never been born.'

Hoofs sounded outside. It was Tex Fortune. Ware called him in. Tex looked grim. 'Better spit on your hands and get ready to throw a few, Logan,' said the grizzled rider. 'I just came in from the Punch Bowl country. There's at least five hundred head of Flat Y cattle being bunched down there just outside our line. That means only one thing. Dobe Yarnell is moving in!'

CHAPTER NINE

THE OMINOUS TIDE

While Ware was at the corrals catching up his favorite buckskin, Tex went over to the bunkhouse after a rifle. He came back with his eyes popping.

'For a minute I think I'm dreaming,' he sputtered. 'Mebbe I am. I go into the bunkhouse. There's a hombre in there, sleepin'. He's got his head all bandaged up. I take a look. And it's Slide Maidlie! Now how in billyblue hell did he get there?'

Ware gave him the story briefly. Tex swore mightily and with satisfaction. 'That means he'll probably side in with us.'

'Not necessarily,' said Ware. 'He don't owe us a thing. Besides, he's a sick man.'

'He won't be sick long,' declared Tex. 'I know Maidlie's breed. They're either dead or they're able to do damage. Takes more than a creased scalp to keep an old he-wolf like Maidlie long in the blankets.'

They were ready to go when a hard-riding figure came spurring in from the west. Tex's eyes narrowed. 'Now what? That's Ed Morlan yonder. He's got a brassbound nerve to come ridin' in here after the way him an' Buck Trubee an' Chain Kelsey acted.'

'Another surprise for you, Tex,' said Ware. 'Ed and Buck are ridin' for us again.'

'The devil they are!' exploded Tex. 'Why, I wouldn't trust them jiggers from here to there.'

'I would, and do,' said Ware. 'They made a mistake, realized it, admitted it. They won't fail that way again. You'll see.'

Morlan pulled his hard-run horse to a sliding stop. He felt Tex's fuming glance and flushed. To Ware he said, 'Buck and me did what you told us, Logan. We stocked up with gear at Jake Farwell's store and then headed for Red Mountain. Out a couple of miles below Guenoc we see a big jag of cattle bein' drifted in from the southwest. We snooker up close enough to read some brands. All Block H stuff. Them Huncutt cows are already over the west line of Hat. Buck stayed to keep an eye on things while I hit gravel for headquarters.'

'Good work, Ed,' said Ware. 'Catch yourself up a fresh bronc. I'll be going back with you. Tex, you take charge down at the Punch Bowl. Send Packy Maroon and Curly Russell over to join up with Ed and Buck and me. You and Rainy and the Larribee boys hold the line at the Punch Bowl. Don't take any fool chances but don't let Dobe Yarnell push you around too much. This is it. They're putting the squeeze on us from east and west at the same time. Scatter!'

Tex raced away and as soon as Ed Morlan switched his saddle to a fresh horse he and

Ware tore off in the opposite direction.

Yeah, thought Ware, this was it! Mize Huncutt and Dobe Yarnell were hitting full out against Hat at last. And shrewdly had they figured their move. You could, Ware realized, fight men, even when the odds were against you. But to fight on-rolling herds of cattle was something else again. Cattle by the hundreds, maybe a thousand in all, driving in on Hat range from two directions at once. They would spread, scatter out, mingle with Hat cows. Then Huncutt and Yarnell could move up still more cattle, push them onto Hat range.

A veritable living tide, flowing up out of the far reaches of Long Valley, spreading across the flats, winding up the gulches, massing on the slopes. Once outside cattle were there, mixed with Hat cattle, eating Hat grass, drinking Hat water, it would take the driving toil of weeks to cut them out and drive them back. And while a man was cutting out and driving off a dozen critters, fifty more could be hazed onto Hat range from some isolated, unguarded section.

This was Hat's biggest weakness—the very size of Hat range. To guard all its borders against tactics like these would require a crew four times the size of the one Logan Ware had available. Yes, there was a malign shrewdness in this blow by Yarnell and Huncutt.

There was dust lifting, far down the valley, a low-lying, tawny brown haze, steadily creeping closer, marking the progress of the tide of cattle. Ware and Ed Morlan picked up Buck Trubee within half a mile of where Morlan had left him.

'It's hard to figure very close, Logan,' reported Trubee. 'But my guess is at least six hundred head in that herd. And maybe half a dozen riders chousin' 'em.'

Ware rode to meet the advancing herd. This particular stretch was winter and spring range, already well grazed off by Hat cattle, which had then moved on, higher up the valley. A few Hat stragglers still hung out here, but not many. The advancing herd was steadily sucking in these stragglers as it advanced.

'They're way over our heads in numbers,' Ware said grimly. 'But we can try and turn them. Come on!'

They lifted to a run, bore down on the point of the herd. Coming closer, Ware saw two pointriders swing wide and race back along the flanks of the herd toward the dust-clouded drag. Ware came in on the point of the herd at an angle and, with swinging riata end and shrill yipping, put on all the pressure he could. On either side of him Ed Morlan and Buck Trubee added their efforts.

For a little time they made progress, drifting the point away, pushing it into the beginnings of a turn. But there were twice the number of men pressing the herd on than were trying to turn it. The herd spun in upon itself, a compressed, milling mass. Then it exploded, away from the point of greatest pressure. Cattle bolted past Ware and his two men despite all they could do, driving them apart, racing between them, then scattering in twos and dozens and scores.

Dust lifted and swirled. Ware lost sight of Ed Morlan and Buck Trubee. His own horse was jostled and driven as the herd, sensing the breaking of a barrier, began to run. It had been a long gamble, trying to turn the herd, and it had lost.

The Huncutt men, driving the cattle, knew what had happened and their lifting yells held both defiance and triumph. Cold temper blazed all through Logan Ware and he fought the jostling cattle bitterly as he tried to break through and get a glimpse of the Block H riders.

Buck Trubee, pushed off to one side, realizing also that the gamble had lost, swung his horse wide, striving to get free of the boiling dust and lunging cattle. Presently the main rush of the cattle was past him and the dust thinned. A mounted figure loomed in front of him. Buck thought it was Ed Morlan.

'Ed,' he yelled, 'what's the next move?'

'This!' came the snarling answer.

Too late did Buck Trubee realize his mistake. This rider in the dust wasn't Ed Morlan. It was Chain Kelsey, and Kelsey, the dark-faced malignant one, was throwing a gun.

Buck Trubee did his best to match Kelsey's draw, but he was way slow. At this close range Kelsey threw two shots. Then, as he spun his horse and sank in the spurs, he spat wickedly, 'Damn turncoat!'

Ed Morlan heard those shots, thudding and heavy above the wild complaint of the harried cattle. Premonition caught at him, laying cold fingers around his heart, pulling his belly muscles into knots. He spurred that way, cursing the dust and the last stragglers of the scattered herd. He caught a glimpse of a rider, racing away. The outline was blurred by the dust, but there was a cast to the head and shoulders of the rider which he knew. Chain Kelsey! Then the dust swirled close again and here was a riderless horse swinging restlessly about, trailing reins.

Logan Ware heard the shots also, but there was nothing he could do about it until he finally fought clear of the acrid dust murk. He had a gun drawn, was alert and ready for anything, more than half expecting a pitched battle then and there with the Block H crowd. He was startled to see them racing away at a hard-driving run, already far beyond short gun range and rapidly drawing beyond anything but the most chancy shooting with a rifle.

Out of the thinning dust burst a rider, dragging at the rifle scabbarded under his stirrup leather. It was Ed Morlan and Ed's face was thin and bitter and reckless. Ware yelled at him, 'No use, Ed—they're gone!'

Ed set his horse up, bounced from the saddle, and dropped to one knee. His rifle crashed and crashed, the echoes running thin and vibrant across the hot sweep of the valley. But his targets were distant, riding low and hard, and Ed swore brokenly when his rifle levered empty with no effect.

Ware pulled over beside him. Ed looked up. 'It's Buck,' he said woodenly. 'Chain Kelsey got him!'

They went back to where Buck Trubee lay. Now the dust was gone and the westering afternoon sunlight burned stark and clear. Both of Chain Kelsey's shots had struck deep and mortally. Ware said tonelessly, 'Get his horse, Ed.'

They had lifted Buck Trubee and laid him across his saddle and were tying him there when the pound of hoofs sounded and Loren Rudd and Lister Beckwith came galloping up. The girl stared at Buck Trubee's limp figure with shocked eyes. 'One of our men? Hurt?' Her voice was tight.

'Dead,' said Ware bleakly.

The girl gasped, caught at her saddle horn with taut, hard-knuckled hands. Ware swung his glance to Beckwith and his voice was rough, and challenging. 'You knew of this plan, maybe? Pushing herds onto Hat grass—trying to drown us with cattle?'

Beckwith shook his head. 'I knew nothing

about it and had no part in it.'

'You could be lying. You were in on their other schemes. You and Huncutt and Yarnell were thick as thieves at one time.' Ware's eyes were polar-bleak.

'That's right,' gritted Ed Morlan. 'It's easy for you to talk, Beckwith. It's harder for me to believe.'

Beckwith shot a hot glance at Ed. 'I'll let that pass, Morlan, only because I understand how you feel right now.'

'You were all with them once and not so long ago,' Ed flared. 'Queer you'd have a change of heart so quick.'

Ware said, 'Let me handle this, Ed.' He swung his horse close beside Beckwith, threw the full impact of searching scrutiny on the man. 'It would be right handy for Yarnell and Huncutt to have a spy ridin' in an' out of Hat headquarters, so they'd know just how we were spread around. Should I get the slightest inkling that's what you're up to, Beckwith—'

'Please!' cut in Loren Rudd. 'It isn't fair to blame Lister for this. He was nowhere around. We just happened to see the cattle and confusion, so rode this way.'

Ware glanced at her, gave a brief nod. He understood now the reason for the retreat of the Block H forces. They had seen the girl and Beckwith coming in at a distance and took them for Hat reinforcements. Also, their main purpose had been achieved, which was to push a Block H herd onto Hat range and scatter it. And for all they knew, more Hat riders might be coming up at any moment.

Ware turned to Ed Morlan. 'We'll get along home. There's nothing we can do about the herd now. It's scattered and here to stay for a while.'

They rode away, leading Buck Trubee's horse. Loren Rudd and Lister Beckwith followed for a while, the girl still and wan of face, Beckwith fuming inwardly, his eyes pinched, his lips taut. Abruptly Beckwith reined in.

'This takes all the edge off the day, Loren. There'll be no welcome at Hat headquarters for me any more. I'll be saying adios, and drifting.'

The girl stirred in her saddle. 'If I wish to welcome you at Hat, it doesn't matter how Logan Ware and the men may feel.'

Beckwith chose his words carefully. 'It's good to hear you say that. I guess you know how much your welcome has come to mean to me. For though a man may guard his words he can't keep his true feelings out of his eyes.'

She met his glance and faint color beat in her cheeks. 'I was enjoying our ride very much—until this dreadful thing took place. You'll come and see me again?'

'If you wish it. In a few days, after this has died down.'

'I'll be looking for you.'

Beckwith watched her ride on, trailing Ware and Ed Morlan and the horse they led, moving slowly under its dread burden. She was very fair, up on that sleek sorrel filly. Even if she were not the owner of the rich Hat properties she was still a prize to quicken the pulse of any man. While, with the Hat ranch—well...

Lister Beckwith's eyes took on a gleaming, mocking avarice. His glance moved up, settled on Logan Ware's departing shoulders. The glance went hot and full of hate. 'I'll let you and Huncutt and Yarnell kill one another off, Ware,' he murmured. 'Then we'll see.'

It was some time before Ware glanced back. When he saw Loren Rudd following alone he let Ed Morlan go on ahead with Buck Trubee's horse, while he pulled in and waited for her. He said, his tone grave, 'Bitter business that you always have to bump into this sort of thing. I'd like to spare you such experiences but it seems I have no choice.'

'Must this sort of thing go on and on?' she burst out. 'Will there never come an end to—to killing?'

Ware shrugged. 'Until covetous men learn to leave Hat interests alone there's no telling what will happen.'

'I think it's making me hate everything about Hat and what it stands for,' she declared fiercely. 'More and more I'm coming to understand how Mother felt.'

Ware made no answer. He had none to give.

They were a mile from headquarters when Packy Maroon and Curly Russell came spurring up. They stared grimly as Ed Morlan rode by, leading Buck Trubee's horse and what it carried. They touched their hats awkwardly to Loren Rudd, who suddenly lifted the sorrel filly to a run and sped out for headquarters. They fell in beside Ware, who explained matters tersely. Then he asked, 'How were things at the Punch Bowl?'

'Flat Y cows all over the place,' answered Packy. 'Yarnell's crowd threw enough pressure in back of their herd to start it running. That was just before Tex got back. Wasn't a thing we could do but get out of the way. The Flat Y crowd didn't stick around and try and make a fight of it. Soon as they saw the herd had got past us, they turned around and drifted. Tex is sitting tight now and wants to know what to do.'

'You go back and tell him and the other boys to come on in to headquarters. This thing is my fault. I've been going a little soft. I should have been hitting instead of waiting. Starting right away, things are going to be different.'

Packy spurred off and Curly Russell dropped in silently beside Ware, who rode in frowning silence.

Yes, thought Ware, he'd pulled a blunder. Because of Loren Rudd, maybe. Trying to shy away from violent action for the sake of her feelings. That had been a mistake, for it had left the initiative in the hands of the enemy. It had been another mistake back there to try and fight cattle, and it had cost the life of a good man. Tex had played it smarter. Tex had let the cattle go.

A man fought in the face of surprise if he had to. But if he didn't have to, if the issue at the moment was not too important, he was smart to give way and wait a better chance. Well, there was one thing about surprise. It could work two ways.

Tex and the rest of the outfit got back to headquarters just after sundown and, in the blue dusk which followed, helped bury Buck Trubee in a little tightly fenced flat a quarter of a mile north of the ranch buildings. Here, under the wide sky, slept Hamp Rudd and several others who had, through the years, worked and fought for Hat. The price of Hat had been high. Now, as they laid Buck Trubee away, another installment had been added to that price.

They ate a quiet supper and then Ware drew Ed Morlan aside. 'You better head for Pete Lord's place and tell him about Buck. He may want to pick up Buck's saddle and other gear. I don't know whether Buck had any closer kin, womenfolks, maybe. I want to find out and maybe Pete can tell me.'

Ed nodded and went over to the corrals. Ware carried some light food over to the bunkhouse. Slide Maidlie was propped up in his bunk, his eyes clear and looking better.

'Be ready for the saddle again pretty quick, Ware,' he said. 'You people have been mighty good to me.'

Ware hunched on the edge of a bunk, smoking silently while the gunman ate. Abruptly he stirred and asked, 'Your gun for sale, Maidlie?'

Maidlie looked at him guardedly, then said, 'No. Not for money. But I might strap it on for a friend. I've never had a real friend and have spent a lot of time wishing I had. Sort of a queer idea for a man like me to have, isn't it?'

'No,' Ware answered slowly. 'Not at all. There's a lot of ice in you, which doesn't make you an easy man to know. Yet you're not a hard man to like.'

Ware rubbed a hand across his face. Somehow there was a weariness in this unconscious gesture, a certain loneliness of spirit. Abruptly he told Maidlie of the happenings of the afternoon, and of the death of Buck Trubee. Then, hardly realizing why, he told the full story behind Hat and what he was trying to do.

Maidlie listened quietly, the beaked fierceness of his face softening slightly. 'You've been making one mistake,' he said finally. 'You haven't been fighting full out. This sort of thing is old stuff to me. I've been through my share of range wars. They're dirty—they're always dirty. And there are no rules. Any man who tries to stick to fair rules gets rubbed out, nine times out of ten. The side that wins hits hardest from the most unexpected angles. You kill men or they'll kill you. You got to be ruthless. You can't brand a cow without scorching hide.'

'A full-out war will be tough on Loren Rudd,' said Ware morosely. 'If things get too rough she might toss up the whole game. She's been close to that idea already. And that ain't what Hamp Rudd wanted. He wanted her to take over Hat—and keep it.'

'She'll lose it anyhow unless you whip that other crowd,' reminded Maidlie, starkly practical. 'She'll either toughen up or she won't. And if she doesn't then she'll never hold Hat now or in the future. There'll always be men who'll look on an outfit as big and rich as Hat as something to slice a chunk out of at any and every chance.'

'In my boots, what would you do?' asked Ware.

The ice came back into Maidlie's eyes. 'Hit the other side and hit them hard. You know your enemy. Go after him, with no holds barred. Put the fear of hell into him. Throw all rules overboard. Go after him!'

'I wish you were riding with us,' said Ware simply. 'Not just as a hired gun fighter, but as one of us. Chousing Hat cows, working for Hat interests, and if necessary, fighting for them.'

A shadowed smile touched Maidlie's stern lips. 'That's simple enough to figure out. Put my name down in your time book at forty and found. That way you'll have hired yourself a hand. But offer me special wages and we can't do business.'

Ware looked into the gunman's cold eyes. 'What did Dave Grande offer you to wipe me out?'

'Five hundred dollars.'

'Yet you turned that down and you'll ride for Hat at forty and found. You're a tough one to figure out, Slide.'

'Ain't I though!' Maidlie's smile went a little twisted and sardonic. 'I can't always figure myself. But then, in some ways I've always been a queer sort of hairpin. Once I thought it was something to walk down the street and know that people were watching me and fearing me and hating me. But hate can get under a man's skin after a time. So right now I want to be an ordinary Hat hand, no more or no less than any of the rest. A deal?'

Ware put out his hand. 'A deal. I hope you stay with us forever, Slide.'

Maidlie said, 'Forever is a long time. Yet the prospect sounds good.'

When Ware left with the empty dishes, Maidlie murmured to himself, 'An ordinary puncher again, at forty and found, riding for a guy who somehow gets under a man's skin. Well, I wouldn't have it different.'

Outside, the rest of the crew were gathered under the stars, smoking and talking in subdued tones, the shadow of Buck Trubee's death still on them. To them Ware said quietly, 'I've just signed on Slide Maidlie at forty and found. He wants to be one of us. Make it so.'

Ware lugged the dishes back to Smoky Atwater's sink, then went over to the ranch house. Loren Rudd answered his knock. Ware said, 'I want to talk with you.'

She followed him out across the patio to the entrance of it, from where the black gulf of the valley lay far and still under their eyes. 'What is it?' asked the girl.

'Starting right away, I'm going to take the gloves off.'

'What do you mean?'

'I'm going all out after those who are hitting at us. It is going to be rough, very rough. No quarter asked and none given. Because of that there is something I must ask of you.'

She was startled at the somber darkness of his tone and mood. 'What is it you want?'

'That you discourage Lister Beckwith from visiting this ranch, and that you don't go riding with him again.'

He could sense the stiffening which ran through her. 'Isn't that being a little ridiculous? What possible harm is there in my riding with Lister?'

'Once Beckwith was one of that other crowd,' said Ware grimly. 'For all I know he still is. His apparent change of heart could be nothing more than a front, so he can spy on us.

And we can't afford to take that chance. There is too much at stake.'

'Perhaps it would simplify things all around if I went back to Canyon to live. There would be no question of anyone spying then.'

Impatience with her rolled suddenly over Ware. He caught her by the arms, his tone harsh. 'That's foolish talk. Is the privilege of riding around with Lister Beckwith of more importance to you than the future of this ranch?'

Bitterness flared in her to match his own. 'I'm trying to make the best of a bad bargain which I did not ask for. I own a ranch, yet I don't—not for a year, anyhow. I have no authority over my own possessions until that year is up. I'm a figurehead and, as such, feel like a fool. I've asked for little enough to bolster my self-respect, just the right to accept the friendship of a man who, as far as I can see, has done Hat no wrong. And who has at all times been a complete gentleman, too much so to ever lay a finger, let alone violent hands on me!'

She twisted, trying to free herself, but Ware's grip tightened. Her tone went icy. 'You presume too much on your authority, Mr Logan Ware. Let me go!'

'Not yet!' Ware's voice was recklessly bitter. 'So Lister Beckwith is a gentleman and I'm not, eh? Maybe you're right. I'm just a damn fool, sticking my stupid neck out as I try and hold this ranch together for you. Buck Trubee died for that same purpose. His thanks? Well, you answer that. While I've been told by more than one that I'll get no thanks either. Yet it's not thanks I want. It's just to make a promise good, I guess. Either that or...'

His words ran out. As he spoke he had unconsciously pulled Loren Rudd closer and closer to him, until now he loomed over her, dark and bitter. Abruptly his head tipped and he kissed her on the mouth.

He set her back from him, and his laugh was harsh with mockery at himself. 'That guarantees me a fool, doesn't it? And no gentleman. But I know now why I haven't been thinking straight.'

He turned and walked away into the night. The girl stood just as he had left her, motionless for a long time. Once she touched a finger to her lips, almost wonderingly.

CHAPTER TEN

WILD NIGHT

The crew was still bunched outside the bunkhouse when Ware came striding up. His words slapped at them, harsh and direct. 'Been a big enough day or do you feel up to a night of riding?'

It was Tex Fortune who got the significance behind Ware's curt words. 'Let's ride,' he drawled. 'Let's ride far and wide, and hit hard. Let's throw a few instead of sitting back and taking it.'

'That,' said Joe Larribee, 'makes sense. Let's ride!'

'Catch and saddle!' ordered Ware.

They broke for the corrals, all eagerness and grim purpose. The somberness of their mood was wiped out in this promise of action.

From inside the bunkhouse sounded Slide Maidlie's voice. 'Hey—Ware!'

Ware went in. 'What's on your mind?'

The gunman's glance was very direct, but not so icily bleak as usual. 'I heard how you put it up to the men. It's a smart move—if you fight smart. Don't give the other side a single break, for they wouldn't give you one. If the luck runs out for some of the boys, don't let it grind you too deep. It's all part of the job. Good luck! In another day or so I'll be riding with you.'

They were ready to go when Ed Morlan and Pete Lord came spurring in out of the night. Ed looked around at the dark mass of men and horses. 'Where'd they hit us this trip, Logan?'

'They haven't. We're going to hand out a few on our own.'

'Good!' said Pete Lord thinly. 'Wait until I throw my war bag under a bunk and I'll be right with you, Ware.'

'This is Hat business, not yours, Pete. Not

that you wouldn't be welcome, you understand.'

'I understand everything,' was Pete Lord's grim reply. 'Ed's given me the story about Buck. Buck was a relation of mine, and a good kid. Not too fast in the head, maybe—but with his heart in the right place. I want,' he ended harshly, 'to get Chain Kelsey over my sights. Be with you in a minute.'

They roared away into the night with Ware thinking, We're even again. We lost Buck, but we got Pete, and there's plenty of rawhide in Pete Lord.

As black distance swallowed up the rush of horses and men, a slim figure came down from the ranch house to the bunkhouse. She was poised in the doorway, fresh and cool in gingham, with lines of troubled thought furrowing her brow. 'How are you feeling?' she asked Slide Maidlie.

The gunman smiled. 'Better, thanks.' And thought to himself that this wasn't what she really wanted to know.

That he was right showed a moment later when Loren Rudd asked, 'What's the trouble now? Where are the men riding to, and what for?'

'In cow country, ma'am,' answered Maidlie, 'when good men ride as Logan Ware and his crew are riding tonight, it's because they've been hurt and are going to hit back at those who've hurt them.'

'I knew it!' she exclaimed. 'I knew he would do something like this. He was born to violence.'

'No,' corrected the gunman gravely, 'no, he wasn't. He was born to love laughter an' peaceful living, the same as any other normal man. He was born to ideals and a strong sense of honor. He was born to be true to a trust and true to his friends. When he uses violence it's because he knows it's the only weapon that'll get results. And the man who hates violence, yet uses it because he has to, is the wickedest fightin' man in the world. I speak with authority, ma'am—because I know considerable about fightin' men.'

'You haven't known Logan Ware very long,' she argued.

'I've known him long enough. We've shaken hands on friendship, him and me. And I rate his friendship as one of the biggest and best things in a life that hasn't known much of either. Remember, whatever he does, he does for this Hat ranch, which means that he's doing it for you too.'

Which left her without any argument at all. She could only say, 'I hate violence and want no more of it, even if it costs me this ranch.'

She went back to the ranch house, walking slowly, knowing that she would sleep poorly this night because it would be one of nagging worry until she heard Logan Ware and his men ride home again.

It was hard to realize that men were riding, vengeance bent, this night. The hush of great space lay over the valley. The sky was black velvet, jeweled with stars. The air was still and warm, but cooling, and the breath of it was of grass, sun-dried and ripe. Sweet air, starlit silence, but the peace was only a mockery, for men were riding, guns ready to their hands.

For her, Logan Ware had said. Slide Maidlie had said that too. So that this Hat ranch would remain for her as her father had left it.

Once or twice she had known a deep stirring of emotion about the ranch, as though pride of ownership were about to establish itself. Yet instinctively she realized that mere possessive pride was not enough. She had to bring more than that to the ranch to be honest on her part. She had to achieve some part of how Logan Ware and his men felt. With them it was a wordless fidelity to Hat.

She had come close to understanding this. Then violence had struck and men had died and everything had left her except revulsion, even hatred for the things Hat stood for, and for which men had to die.

Along with her material heritage there was a spiritual something which she had as yet been unable to grasp. As she slipped into the ranch house and went quietly to her room she had the disturbed feeling that perhaps she wasn't measuring up to big responsibilities.

Back to her came the picture of Logan Ware

as he had loomed above her out there at the patio entrance. Even yet her arms ached from the steely grip of his hands. And her lips—where he had kissed her—burned. She pressed her hands against her cheeks, felt the heat of the flush still there...

Through the night Logan Ware and the Hat crew rode east, their horses pulled down from that first driving run to a more practical pace. East they continued until ahead and to their slight left the lights of Guenoc pin-pointed the night. Then they began swinging south until finally another small cluster of lights lifted out of the black gulf before them. The Block H headquarters. Mize Huncutt's layout.

Logan Ware reined in. 'I know how you feel, boys—for I feel the same way,' he said briefly. 'You'd like to barge right in down there and clean house. We could probably do it, but some of us wouldn't come out alive. Which might weaken Hat to a point where Dobe Yarnell could move in and smash us. So we use our heads and give Huncutt something to worry about. We'll ride two circles and shoot things up. When I give the long yell we'll gather and be on our way. To Canyon. A hombre there I want to talk to. All set?'

Ware slid his rifle out of its saddle boot, lifted his horse to a run, and in a long, curving line the rest of the outfit followed. Ware swooped in until the lights were not glowing flecks hanging disembodied in the blackness, but instead resolved into squares and rectangles of lighted windows in bunkhouse and ranch house. Then he threw up his rifle and began to shoot.

The bunkhouse was closest so he gave that half the contents of his rifle's magazine. The other half he poured into the ranch house proper, pulling for those lighted windows. When the gun clicked empty he was past the ranch house, so swung circling to the right, stuffing fresh ammunition through the loading gate of his weapon.

Behind him came his men, shooting as he had done, searching every cranny of Huncutt's headquarters with whistling lead. It was blind shooting to a large extent, but it was not difficult to visualize the consternation going on in the buildings with rifle slugs smashing through windows and walls, splintering and gouging timber and joist.

Faint above the crash and snarl of guns came a thin, enraged yelling. Whirling around on his second circle, Ware cut in sharply toward the now dark buildings. He knew this layout and he raced up to the cavy corral. Leaning low in his saddle, he slid back the locking bar, let the corral gate swing wide. Then he was gone again, riding low and hard.

Guns began to spit crimson from the dark mass of the buildings. Block H had recovered from the first confusion and surprise and was beginning to fight back. So now Ware shot at these gun flares, as did those following him. When he came around again he pulled in, cupped a hand about his mouth, and gave the long yell.

They came racing up to him through the dark, these men of his, and he knew a deep relief when they all checked in, untouched and exultant. There was a massed pounding of hoofs bursting through the night to their left and Curly Russell exclaimed, 'We got 'em up and riding! Things can get real interestin', now.'

'Not riding, Curly,' said Ware. 'That's their cavy herd runnin' wild. I went in and opened the corral gate. It'll be daylight or better before they'll get hold of a saddle bronc.'

'I doubt we did 'em any real harm,' said Tex Fortune. 'But we sure spoiled their night's sleep and gave 'em something to think about. Also, it'll cost Mize Huncutt a penny or two for new windows an' that'll gripe his miserly soul. Hamp Rudd would have enjoyed this little soiree.'

'Every time I cut loose,' said Pete Lord harshly, 'I was prayin' my lead would go right down Chain Kelsey's throat. Listen to 'em, will you? They're still shootin' holes in an empty night.'

Ware reined away, setting his bronc's head toward town. He felt better. Some of the bitter frustration that had banked up in him was gone. While, as Tex had said, this raid had probably done little real damage to the enemy it had accomplished one thing. It had brought everything out into the open. Jockeying for position, false and nerve-draining peace were all done with. From now on the enemy would know what they could expect any time and anywhere. This, it seemed, was what they wanted. Open war, outfit against outfit, with no mercy asked or given. This was grim battle, a fight to the finish. This was the way Hamp Rudd would have had it, rough, roaring and defiant.

It meant that every man must ride with his rifle across his saddle. Yet that was better than being at half measures. If Huncutt and Dobe Yarnell had hoped to strangle Hat with the sheer weight of cattle alone and settle the issue by that means, they were going to be disappointed. This night would show them that they'd have to shoot their way through. And maybe they wouldn't like that way of things too much.

Canyon was quiet when they rode in. Ware led the way straight to the Empire. He went in with his men crowding at his heels.

Stubby Hoffmeyer and Jake Farwell were at a table playing cribbage. At another Ace Tomlin, the house gambler, had a game going with two Flat Y riders, Jenkins and Pardee, and with Black Tom Gaddy, who had come over from Guenoc for a change of scene. Dave Grande was busy behind the bar.

Ware jerked his head toward the poker players and said over his shoulder to Tex Fortune, 'Keep an eye on that crowd and don't let any of them leave. I'll get around to them later on.'

Ware stopped by the cribbage players. 'Hi, Stubby—Jake! How you peggin'?'

Farwell, never a friendly man, merely grunted and did not look up, intent on his play. But Stubby leaned back and grinned up at Ware, though the grin faded somewhat when he glimpsed the driven rashness in Ware's eyes.

'Good enough, Logan,' he said. 'And you?'

Ware's smile pulled thin and hard across his teeth. 'Out on a chore to separate the sheep from the goats, Stubby. Watch yourself if things turn rough. Wouldn't be interested in buying out Grande, would you?'

Stubby's chin dropped. 'Huh? Wh—what? Dave ain't figgerin' on sellin' out, is he?'

'He will be, damn shortly.'

Ware went on to the bar, looked into Dave Grande's cold, hard eyes, and said bluntly, 'You got an hour to close up your affairs and get out of town, Grande.'

Grande, mechanically swabbing down the bar, went dead still, then said, his voice flatly even, 'That's a lousy joke, Ware.'

'No joke. Cold turkey!'

Watching closely, Ware saw Grande's eyes dilate, let out a red glare, then narrow to a masked blankness again. It was as if a window had been momentarily opened to disclose a blazing pit beyond. 'You're crazy,' gritted the saloon owner. 'Or drunk!'

'Cold sober and sane,' retorted Ware. 'And tired of letting your kind run loose. I think the first time you ever laid eyes on me, Grande—you hated my guts. Which makes us even. But I was willing to live and let live. Different with you, though. You wanted my scalp. You brought in Slide Maidlie and offered him five hundred dollars to push me into a corner and smoke me down. Slide happens to be a pretty square hombre, though, and turned you down. So you tried to have him dry-gulched, and only came close. Slide's riding for Hat now. Why, I'm really doing you a favor, giving you a chance to skip the country before Slide Maidlie is able to be up and in a saddle again. What do you imagine would happen to you if you ever met up with Slide again?'

Dave Grande's hands, spread on the bar top, went white and the finger tips splayed with the pressure put on them. Little ridges of taut muscle quivered and crawled along his swarthy jaw. Despite the malevolent taciturnity of the man he could not fully hide the tempest of feeling that racked him. 'Your imagination,' he blurted hoarsely, 'is runnin' away with you.'

'Imagination doesn't figure in at all,' Ware said curtly. 'Just cold facts. You're wasting part of that hour.'

'And suppose I don't go?'

'You'll go. On your own two feet—or on a board. Now I'm through arguin'. Make up your mind!'

'That's right,' said a voice at Ware's elbow. 'Make up your mind, Grande.'

It was Pete Lord, lank and leathery, harsh as weathered stone. 'It was a pretty good valley while Hamp Rudd was alive,' went on Pete. 'A man could sort of relax and figure ahead. The minute Hamp died there came a difference. The snakes began crawlin' out from under the leaves. Hat looked like a fat carcass and the varmints began to gather for the feast. Well, it happens that some of us realize the worth of Hat as a good, solid balance in Long Valley. We aim to keep it so. We can do without the snakes and the varmints, but not without Hat.'

Ware laughed, without mirth. 'You see how it is, Grande?'

'You're asking the impossible,' burst out Grande, his voice pinched and strangled in his throat. 'You can't do this to me.'

'And you can't go on scheming to have men shot in the back,' said Ware remorselessly. 'First Tilton Bennett—no man to be trusted, maybe. But there's a principle of sorts there. Maybe you called that move, maybe you didn't. But I'm sure of my ground where Slide Maidlie is concerned. You wanted my scalp, Grande—were willing to pay five hundred dollars for it. You think I'm fool enough to give you a second chance? Hardly! You're wasting precious time. Think fast. Make Stubby Hoffmeyer an offer. Maybe he'll buy you out.'

By this time every man in the room was listening. The poker game was forgotten. Black Tom Gaddy got up and came over to the bar. 'Ain't you bein' awful rough on Dave, Ware?' he growled. 'He's all right.'

Ware looked Gaddy up and down. 'That places you, right where I figured you'd be. Get back to Guenoc and stay there and mind your business damn close and quiet, Gaddy—or you'll be taking the long ride too.'

'I'll go where I please, when I please and—'

Gaddy broke off short as Curly Russell jabbed a hard elbow into his ribs. 'You'll do as you're told, mister,' said Curly. 'Remember me? I'm the guy you and your crooked table euchred out of maybe a hundred and fifty pesos one night in Guenoc not so long ago. You were the tough hombre that night. Well, I'm the tough hombre this night. You got your ridin' orders. Take 'em and git!'

Curly's blue eyes were full of a taunting recklessness. Black Tom Gaddy didn't hold the hand he had at Guenoc. It wasn't three or four to one now in Gaddy's favor. He looked around and said, 'I never bet against a pat hand.'

He looked across the bar at Grande and said, 'They're holding all the aces, Dave. This deal is sour.'

Gaddy turned and went out. Curly Russell followed him and watched from the shadow outside the door until Gaddy had swung into his saddle and spurred out of town.

Dave Grande seemed to have got hold of himself, for he shrugged abruptly, looked over at Stubby Hoffmeyer, and said, 'How much you offer me for the layout, Hoffmeyer?'

Stubby, bewildered by it all, began to stutter. Finally he got out, 'I don't want no saloon. I got a hotel already and that keeps me busy. No, I don't want no saloon.'

Jake Farwell said abruptly, 'Twenty-five hundred—cash.'

Grande said, 'Worth twice that much. Talk sense, Farwell.'

'Twenty-five hundred,' repeated Farwell. 'Not one thin dime more.'

'That,' said Ware, 'is a lot more than nothing, Grande.'

Grande gnawed a lip to whiteness, then shrugged. 'A damn holdup, all the way through. But I got no choice.'

Jake Farwell headed for the door. 'I'll be back with the money inside of ten minutes.'

'Which will just give you time to get your war bag packed, Grande,' said Ware.

Dave Grande slept in a room in back of the barroom. He took a small lamp off the bottle shelf, lighted it, opened the door of the back room. Ware and Pete Lord followed him in.

Alertness immediately stiffened Ware, his

nostrils crinkling. Fresh cigarette smoke was in the air. The blankets on the single bunk were rumpled. Ware stepped over, dropping a hand on them. They were warm. Someone had been lying on that bunk not too long before. Ware, trying the rear door of the room, found it unlocked. He turned on Dave Grande.

'Who was in this room?'

Grande's eyes were blank. 'I don't know. If I did I wouldn't say. There's a limit to how much you can push me around, Ware.'

Ware said, 'Watch him, Pete.' Then he hurried out into the barroom and to the street. Tex Fortune followed him, asking, 'What's up?'

'Not sure anything is. I just want to make a little prowl. Be back in a minute or two.'

The street lay black and empty, the gloom particularly deep on the east side where the row of poplar trees marched in graceful but ghostly silhouette against the distant stars. Ware slid along through this blackness, from tree to tree, pausing every few steps to keen the night.

There was a queer rippling along his spine, as though the fingers of prescience were ruffling his nerve ends. He tried to add this thing up. Somebody who could have overheard all that went on in the barroom had definitely been in that back room of the Empire, and he had slipped out of the room just before Grande led the way into it.

Downstreet a faint yellow glow flickered, then held steady. Ware identified it as a light in

Jake Farwell's store. Which meant that Farwell was probably opening his safe, getting the money he had offered Grande for the Empire.

Ware moved down that way, staying off the board sidewalk, using the deep pawed dust along the hitch rails to muffle his cautious steps, while the black tree shadows hid the tall, alert shape of him. Again and again he swung his head, trying to get at the answer of that grinding uneasiness.

The lamplight in Jake Farwell's store blinked out, a door grated closed, and then Ware heard the storekeeper coming up along the board sidewalk, putting down his heels in that measured, emphatic way he had.

Farwell was just passing the mouth of the alley that ran back from the street past the corner office that had been that of Tilton Bennett. Now there was a swift rush, a blur of violent movement, a snarling curse, a muffled blow, and then the thump of a falling body.

The whole thing was twenty feet away from Ware. He ducked under a hitch rail, snapped out his gun, leaped forward. A startled curse met him, and the impression of a shadowy figure springing upright and whirling toward him, then floundering and stumbling and falling directly at him. Ware could have shot, but didn't, instead chopping down with the heavy barrel of his gun. The blow landed glancingly and then clawing hands were grabbing at Ware, who warded them off with his free arm while smashing out with his gun a second time. This time the blow landed solidly and the floundering figure collapsed in a heap at Ware's feet.

From the dark in back of Ware, Tex Fortune said, 'You take too many chances, boy. If that jigger hadn't stepped off the edge of the sidewalk when he whirled, he'd have plugged you. Who is it?'

Ware said gruffly, 'You damned old Indian! I never heard you come up.'

Ware stripped a match from a block of 'sulphurs,' slid the head of it across the leg of his jeans. The match snapped into flame and Ware cupped it in his hands a moment, then bent over. Tex, peering past his shoulder, swore softly.

'Chain Kelsey!'

Kelsey was out cold. In one hand he held a thick wad of currency.

In the middle of the sidewalk Jake Farwell was mumbling and cursing, trying to get to his feet, managing to rear up on one knee, then spilling over again. Ware stepped beside him and said, 'Take it easy, Jake. Everything is all right now.'

Farwell mumbled brokenly, 'Saw him duck outa the alley at me and got part way clear before he took a swipe at me. But he got hold enough to drop me. Then he grabbed my money ... Where's the money?'

'Right here, Jake. Easy, fellah—easy!'

With Ware aiding him the storekeeper struggled to his feet. 'Who was it?' Farwell wanted to know.

'Chain Kelsey.'

'Kelsey! Well, he allus did look like a bad one to me. How'd he know I had big money on me?'

'He was in the back room of the Empire, Jake. He heard what went on in the barroom and when you headed for your store after the money he sneaked out the back way and laid for you in the alley.'

'This town!' groaned Farwell, feeling carefully of his bruised head. 'More damn crooks ...!'

'This one's beginnin' to stir,' drawled Tex. 'He's all rattler and I ought to stomp him.'

'Shake him to his feet and bring him along,' said Ware. 'I want to ask Mr Dave Grande about this.'

With Ware helping him, Jake Farwell clattered along the sidewalk to the Empire. Behind, half pushing, half dragging his man, Tex came along with Chain Kelsey.

In the Empire, Dave Grande was standing at the inner end of the bar, an old canvas gripsack of personal belongings on the bar beside him. As Ware steered Jake Farwell through the door of the place and the light of the hanging lamps showed Farwell's dazed face with a smear of blood seeping down it, a mutter of surprise ran all through the room and all eyes centered on the storekeeper.

Then, when Tex Fortune appeared, shoving the shambling Chain Kelsey in front of him, that mutter of surprise became a growl. Pete Lord, standing closest to Dave Grande, exclaimed, 'Chain Kelsey, by God! That's the whelp I want!' Pete moved up along the bar toward the renegade puncher.

For the moment all eyes were on Kelsey, including Dave Grande's, and into Grande's black, cold orbs leaped a flame of desperation and resolve. He whirled and darted back into the rear room, slamming and locking the door. Then he was across this room and out the back door, two long strides ahead of the slug which Pete Lord sent crashing through the thin wall after him.

Swearing in bitter disgust, Pete smashed a shoulder against that locked door, but the lock held up. Ware yelled, 'Stay right with Kelsey, Tex!' Then he was out the front of the saloon with Rainy Day, Ed Morlan, and Curly Russell.

They circled the Empire and found nothing, 'Spread out and look for him!' Ware ordered. 'He can't be far.'

They searched the night, but the blackness was all against them and presently, clear out at the edge of town, they heard the sudden pound of racing hoofs, quickly fading.

Ware heard Rainy Day growl in baffled

anger. 'No use, Rainy,' he called. 'He's gone. Which was what we wanted, anyhow.'

'He didn't make the break until Tex brought Kelsey in,' said Rainy. 'Which proves to me that if we could have put 'em face to face we might have learned some answers.'

'We'll get the answers anyhow,' Ware said briefly.

They gathered back in the Empire. Tex had Chain Kelsey sitting in a chair. Kelsey's dark face was more malevolent than ever. The happenings of the night had stripped away every thin veneer and Chain Kelsey was definitely all wolf, surly, snarling, and venomous.

At the poker table, where they had sat quietly through everything, Jenkins and Pardee, the Flat Y riders, and Ace Tomlin, the house tinhorn, eyed Ware uncertainly as he came over to them.

'I don't know how deep you two figure to sit in with Dobe Yarnell or how far you'll stretch the string for him,' said Ware to the two riders. 'Yarnell has started things, so what the Flat Y gets it's asked for. It won't be nice and it won't be easy. You can make your choice—now!'

The two riders stirred restlessly. Jenkins blurted, 'You mean we can drift the country or take the consequences?'

'That's the general idea. Which will it be?'

Pardee shrugged. 'There's a limit to how much trail you can take in, Ware. You can't run everybody out of the country who don't agree with you.'

'I can make a hell of a good try at it. Put your guns on the table!'

They stared at him a moment, then did as ordered. Ware picked up the weapons and turned to Ace Tomlin. 'You're out of a job, Tomlin.'

'I know that,' Tomlin replied. 'You'll get no argument from me there, Ware. The world's a big place and I can stand to see a lot of it.'

Ware nodded. 'The stage will be through tomorrow. Take it!'

He turned. 'Curly, go get that jumper off my saddle.'

Curly was soon back with the garment. Ware held it in front of Kelsey. 'Recognize that?'

Kelsey merely cursed.

'It's yours, of course, and you know it,' said Ware. 'This jumper was picked up the other morning out by the lake shore, where our drift fence had been cut and a bunch of Hat cows choused out into the mud to die. Killing cattle that way, or stealing them, all amounts to the same thing. I don't know who else was there with you, Kelsey—but I do know you were there. That's the first count.'

The room was very still. All present sensed something stern and implacable in the making, a rendering of bitter judgment. Even the working and snarling of Kelsey's face blanked out to a set, hard glare.

'Then,' went on Ware remorselessly, 'then there was Buck Trubee. Buck was a good boy who you tried to lead wrong, Kelsey. When you couldn't, you killed him. Yet once you rode with him and called him friend. That's the second count.'

'That's the big count with me,' growled Pete Lord.

'Then there is tonight's little affair,' went on Ware grimly. 'You were hid out in the back room, Kelsey—and you listened to what went on in here. You heard Jake Farwell say he was going after twenty-five hundred dollars, so you went and laid for him, gun-whipped him, and tried to rob him. That's the third count.'

'All of which gets us—where?' snarled Kelsey.

Ace Tomlin had been staring at Kelsey, a thinly mocking smile on his gambler's face. He lifted a hand and fingered the dark flush of a bruise on the side of his face. Now he said, 'None of my business of course, Ware—but while you're at it, why not ask him about Tilton Bennett?'

Kelsey jerked around in his chair. 'You damned tinhorn! Keep your mouth shut! I slugged you once for—'

'That's just it,' cut in Tomlin. 'You slugged me, Kelsey. You knocked me down and while I was down you kicked me around and cussed me out pretty wicked. You were a tough dog then, Kelsey. Now it's my turn. Yeah, Ware—ask him who shot the lawyer in the back and who tried to dry-gulch that gun fighter, Slide Maidlie. Oh, Mr Kelsey has been the busy little bee and no mistake.'

Chain Kelsey gathered himself as though to leap from his chair, but Tex Fortune grabbed him by the shoulder and rasped, 'Stay put! Things do catch up with a man, Kelsey.'

Logan Ware looked at Ace Tomlin, a certain contempt in his glance. Tomlin flushed.

'These things done at Dave Grande's orders, Tomlin?' Ware asked. 'The Bennett affair, I mean—and the try for Maidlie?'

Rubbing his hands in a little circle on the table top, Tomlin shrugged. 'Grande treated me all right. I don't know what you're talking about.'

There was no need of any more answers, thought Ware. The thing answered itself, now. It was Tomlin's chance to get even with Chain Kelsey for some past mistreatment. And while Tomlin had the grace not to inform openly on Dave Grande, he had, with what he had disclosed concerning Kelsey, as deeply damned Grande. For there was no purpose in Kelsey shooting Tilton Bennett in the back except under orders from someone, or in lying in wait along the trail for Slide Maidlie by the same direction.

Ware looked all around the room, met the glances of his men. 'All right, boys,' he said wearily. 'We'll vote on this. Pete, you first. Buck Trubee was a relation of yours. What's your vote?'

'Hang him!' rapped Pete Lord harshly. 'That's the only medicine for a murderer, a traitor, and a cow thief.'

Ware looked at Ed Morlan. 'Buck was your bunkie, Ed. What's your say?'

'Pete Lord spoke for me,' said Ed quietly.

'Pete spoke for all of us, Logan,' said Tex Fortune. 'This is no time to go soft.'

One by one Ware met the eyes of his men and got their affirming nods. 'All right,' he said. 'There's that old cottonwood just outside of town.'

He turned to Jenkins and Pardee, the two Flat Y hands. 'Made up your minds?'

Jenkins licked his lips, jerked a nod. 'We'll drift.'

'That's a promise,' said Ware. 'Don't break it.'

Pete Lord said, 'Put Kelsey on my horse.'

They went down the dark and silent street. They stopped under the ancient cottonwood. Pete Lord and Tex Fortune tied Kelsey's wrists, looped a rope about his neck, tossed the free end over a limb, and tied it solidly to the trunk of the tree.

Logan Ware said, 'Anything you want to say, Kelsey?'

His only answer was a flood of blistering, raging curses.

Pete Lord whistled and his horse walked ahead. The cottonwood limb creaked and swayed with the sudden weight transferred to it and the fluttering of its leaves set up a dreary, rustling sound.

CHAPTER ELEVEN

BITTER AWAKENING

Gray dawn was less than an hour away when Loren Rudd, waking from a fitful sleep, heard Logan Ware and his crew ride in. She listened at her open window, heard the slap of leather as latigos were loosened and drawn from cinch rings, heard a horse spin its bit ring, heard another sigh wearily as the saddle burden was lifted from its back. Heard the clink of spurs and a low murmured word or two.

Little sounds, coming through the dark air of early morning. But no light came on in the bunkhouse, which would have been the case had a wounded man been brought in.

Loren went back to sleep and did not waken again until bright sunlight poured in through her window. She heard unusual movement going on in the house, so jumped up and dressed swiftly. She went out to find a big freight wagon drawn up in front of the patio and Mother Sutton supervising the unloading and bringing in of various items of furniture. Mother Sutton introduced her to a brawny, open-faced young fellow.

'My son Steve,' Mother Sutton said.

Logan Ware was there, with a couple of the hands, helping. He was grave and silent, looking a trifle gaunt. Loren got him aside.

'Last night—none of our men were hurt?'

'Not a scratch,' he told her.

The answer did not wholly satisfy her, for there was something about him which hinted at things untold. He moved off to give a lift with a piece of particularly heavy furniture.

Loren ate breakfast alone and from the kitchen window saw Ware talk briefly with Steve Sutton, who left soon atop his heavy freight wagon. Riders began catching and saddling and riding off in pairs.

Ware came over to the office alone. Loren went in a little later and found him slouched in his chair, staring grim-faced at nothing.

'Are you sure you told me the truth?' she asked. 'You said none of our men were hurt last night. Yet something is troubling you. What is it?'

He hesitated, looking at her guardedly. 'The question of right and wrong has got me by the throat. The boys all say we did right. I'm not so sure.' He drew a deep breath. 'Last night we voted to hang a man.'

There, he thought, that does it. She'll hate me forever and ever now. But it is better for her to find it out from me than from someone else.'

She caught the back of a chair, leaned on it, slim hands white with pressure.

'You—hanged a man—last night?'

'Yes. Chain Kelsey. The man who helped cut our drift fence at the lake and drove cows through it to die in the mud. The man who killed Buck Trubee and who shot Tilton Bennett in the back. The man who tried to gulch Slide Maidlie and tried to rob Jake Farwell. Those are the things I know of. There could have been and probably were more. So—we hung him.'

He could see something almost like physical sickness come over her. She spoke as though to herself.

'I've tried to understand that—that a man might kill in defense of his own life. And that a rider might die as Buck Trubee did, in open fight over range and cattle. But to order a man hanged! Only the law may do that. No one else has the right.'

The look she gave him made him cringe. He would rather have taken a cut from a quirt across the face.

'That's just it,' he said tonelessly. 'If there was any law in this valley—any court...' Then he went on, almost defiantly, 'What would you have had us do? Turn Kelsey loose to do more deviltry? The man was all renegade and guilty as any man ever could be. We did what we felt was right.'

'But you had no right—no right at all!' She was flaying him now. 'You are not the law. You're not a king. There's savagery in you. I've felt it from the first. Don't tell me you do such things for me—for my interests! You do them because there's a brute in you, a brute that I despise!'

She turned and ran from the room.

Ware got to his feet, paced the room. 'You put a load on me, Hamp,' he muttered. 'And I don't know if I can stand up to it. Maybe I'm not the man, after all.'

There was a sodden, bone-deep weariness in him, more mental than physical, and along with this was a biting restlessness. He went back to the bunkhouse and met Slide Maidlie coming out of it. Aside from a certain gauntness, Maidlie seemed much his old self. His hat hid most of the bandage on his head.

Maidlie grinned. 'A man like me can stand just so much bunk. I'm going to catch up Cougar and hit a saddle again for a while. I'm restless.'

'That makes a pair of us,' nodded Ware. 'Come on.'

They went over to the corrals, caught and saddled and headed out.

Back in the ranch house, Mother Sutton was trying to get Loren Rudd interested in placing the new furnishings. The girl was apathetic.

Mother Sutton, the soul of patience, finally lost hers.

'I declare I don't understand you, Loren Rudd!' she burst out. 'Here the biggest ranch in Long Valley is yours. This ranch house is the finest building anywhere around. Your future is bright, or could be if you wished to make it so. You have a devoted foreman and crew. You should be the happiest person alive. Instead you are moody and dissatisfied. What on earth's the matter with you?'

The girl's mouth and chin set in their old lines of severity. There was defiance in the glance she turned on Mother Sutton.

'You do not know that last night this devoted foreman you speak of helped to—hang a man.'

'I know all about it,' declared Mother Sutton. 'Logan told me about it himself. So did Steve, my own son. Logan did more than that. He ran that evil-eyed saloon owner, Dave Grande, out of town. Bless the boy for both things.'

'Now I don't understand you!' Loren said sharply. 'How can you, a woman, say that? I mean—about the hanging? Such a ghastly thing!'

Mother Sutton dropped a hand on Loren Rudd's arm, pulled her over to a brand-new sofa.

'Sit down here with me, my dear. Once I was young, like you, and full of the same kind of ideas about life and death, right and wrong, justice and injustice. This country then was much wilder, much rougher, much more brutal than now. There were good men and bad men, there were honest men and there were thieves. There were truths and there were lies. And if the good men had not been stronger and more enduring than the bad, then Long Valley would today be a howling wilderness. I'm remembering your father, when I first knew him.'

'Why do you and Logan Ware always come back to my father?' demanded the girl.

'Because,' said Mother Sutton simply, 'in his way he was a great man. Do you know what his home was when he first came to Long Valley? Just a burrow in the earth. A dugout, cut into the slope of a hill, roofed with cottonwood branches and sod, a cubby hardly as big as the pantry of this ranch house. That was Hampton Rudd's start. To that start he brought courage, fortitude, faith. And whatever ruthlessness that was necessary. He worked and fought and worked some more. And he built, acre by acre, stone by stone.

'Men not even one half his worth in character and courage and strength tried again and again to smash him, destroy him and all his works. One by one he whipped them. Those who needed killing, he killed. Those who deserved hanging, he hung. Those who deserved to be run out of the country, he ran. He made Long Valley a fit place for decent people to live. Hampton Rudd and his breed of men opened the wilderness of the West, made its future secure. Sometimes I think the Lord fashioned men like that for that express purpose.'

Mother Sutton's kindly eyes seemed to deepen with the light of past glories.

'I'm glad,' she went on, 'that I was able to be a part of such times. At first I was much like you are now, revolted by the raw brutality which broke loose now and then. But I came to realize that life and death did not matter so much as long as it was the good who lived and the evil who died. Chain Kelsey was a slinking wolf. He deserved what he got. It took more courage than you realize to hang him, for that meant accepting a great responsibility. Not all people had the courage for that. Logan Ware has it because he is made of the same stuff as Hampton Rudd. The strong of the West.'

Loren sat stiffly erect. 'He could have run Chain Kelsey out of the valley the same as he did that saloonkeeper. But to hang a man...'

'To have ordered Kelsey out of the valley wouldn't have kept him out. He'd have come slinking back, to prowl and kill some more. You don't order evil things like Kelsey out of this life. You stamp them out.'

The stubbornness that was in the girl did not soften. Seeing this, Mother Sutton sighed deeply and stood up.

'I'm afraid, my dear, that there are some things you are going to have to learn the hard way. It won't be pleasant, and I would like to spare you the experience if I could. But maybe that's the best way.'

Mother Sutton went off about her housework. The girl sat for some time moodily. Then she got up and went into the office. This little room reflected the personality of one man, Logan Ware. Tally books stacked neatly on the desk and the ranch time book beside them. She idly turned the pages of this last. The writing in it was not smooth and cultured, yet there was a certain strength, a definiteness to each letter.

A name leaped off a page at her. Chain Kelsey. She shut the book quickly. There it was, the damning evidence. Once this man Kelsey had ridden for Hat. Once he had slept in the same bunkhouse, eaten at the same table with Logan Ware, ridden with him on the same ranch chores. A chill ran through Loren. Regardless of what Kelsey had done, to have taken him out and hanged him...

She went to the window and saw Lister Beckwith riding in past the corrals. She darted to the door and out to meet him. Here was one man at least, in this wild valley, who seemed to have time and the wish for the gentler, quieter things of life. It would be a vast relief to ride with him, talk with him.

Beckwith saw the eagerness in her eyes and smiled as he took off his hat.

'I was a little doubtful of my welcome,

Loren,' he said. 'Expected any minute to bump into some tough, scowling hombre. But I took the chance, for I couldn't stay away. That's how I feel about you, Loren.'

The warmth of his words sent a faint flush across her face.

'You've no idea how glad I am to see you, Lister,' she said. 'I want to get away from here for a while. Will you catch and saddle Cherry for me while I go change?'

He reached for his rope with alacrity. 'Will I!'

Beckwith had just finished saddling the little sorrel filly and was slipping the headstall into place when Smoky Atwater came shuffling over from the cookshack, looking grim.

'You still own a ranch, Beckwith?' asked Smoky.

'Of course I do. That's a fool question.'

'Couldn't help but wonder. What with everybody else in the valley doin' a heap of scramblin' to hold things together, you seem to be the lone juniper with time to do a lot of hangin' around.'

Anger glinted in Beckwith's eyes. 'I tend to my own affairs. Suppose you tend to yours, Atwater.'

'Loren Rudd is my affair, Beckwith,' bristled Smoky. 'You go ridin' with that girl, you got a heap of responsibility on your hands. Don't you ever forget that—because I won't. Neither will Logan Ware.'

Smoky turned and went back. Beckwith stared after him, eyes fuming.

'There'll come a day,' he muttered, 'when you and a lot of others like you will go down the trail wondering what hit you.'

Beckwith was smiling again when Loren came hurrying from the ranch house, dressed for riding.

'Where away?' he asked as they started out.

She pointed in the direction of Red Mountain.

'I've never been that way.'

The sorrel wanted to run so she let it have its way for half a mile, before reining down to a jog and letting Beckwith catch up. The action flushed her face and cleared some of the moodiness from her eyes.

'I feel better,' she said. 'Like I was free of some prison full of awful shadows.'

'That's no way to feel about your own ranch,' said Beckwith. 'Or maybe it ain't the ranch, but just the people? I can see you've been hearing things. About Chain Kelsey, I mean. I wouldn't want that on my conscience.'

Loren was startled to hear herself saying, 'Maybe it was justified. Maybe Kelsey deserved it.'

'Maybe. But not at the judgment of a mob. But let's not talk about unpleasant things. Let's talk about you and me.'

She looked at him and saw much that could be pleasing to a woman's eye. He had good shoulders, his features were regular and handsome, and his teeth flashed white when he smiled. He flashed that smile at her now.

'Do I pass muster?'

'You've been good to me,' she admitted slowly. 'You seem to understand me better than any of the rest. You can see my side of things.'

'I'd like to put in the rest of my life, Loren—understanding you, seeing things your way so that you'd be happy.'

She looked away, frowning, troubled. 'Maybe I don't see things clearly, Lister. Maybe the fault is all mine. I would want to be sure of that before I could be sure of anything else. I came here with certain ideas concerning my ranch. Now I'm not sure those ideas were right. I'm quite a mixed-up person, it would seem.'

She lifted the sorrel to a lope and the miles fell away under the little filly's light spurning hoofs. Beckwith kept pace with her, content to respect her mood for the moment. This, he knew, was a hand which would require very careful playing. One slightest wrong move could spoil everything.

They passed cattle, Hat cattle and Square H cattle. Here was range over which the tide of Mize Huncutt's cattle invasion had washed. Not far from this very spot was where Chain Kelsey had shot down Buck Trubee. But the girl did not know this nor did she seem to read any significance in these mixed brands of the cattle around them.

Beckwith did not miss it, however. And he realized that his time was not here yet, that he'd have to be patient. Not until Mize Huncutt and Dobe Yarnell and Logan Ware had destroyed or weakened each other to virtual helplessness would his turn come.

The slow turn of the range broke here into a gully, cut by winter storms, now dry and scabbed with whitened gravel. The short angle of trail which dropped steeply into it was cut deep with dust which lifted in an amber haze about them as their horses churned through it. They bent their heads, momentarily blinded. And when the dust cleared they found themselves facing five mounted men!

The one in the lead, left arm in a sling, with hard and bloodshot eyes, was Mize Huncutt. Two of those with him were Morry Seever and Spade Orcutt. The other two were Fred Harmon and Milo Kron.

Loren Rudd, slightly in the lead, reined in, startled. Then something swelled up in her, a certain instinctive fear. For Mize Huncutt said, voice heavy and harsh, 'This is real luck. Get 'em both, boys!'

Loren tried to swing the filly and cut back along the trail. But Lister Beckwith's horse was blocking the way and before Loren could get clear it was Morry Seever who spurred up and grabbed her rein. And it was Fred Harmon who was alongside of Lister Beckwith, the naked gun in his hand jammed hard against Beckwith's middle. With his other hand, Harmon reached over and lifted Beckwith's gun.

Beckwith sat utterly still, his face draining white, while he stared at something he saw in Mize Huncutt's eyes. Huncutt laughed mirthlessly and said, 'You damn slickery, double-crossing whelp! Who did you think you were fooling, anyhow? Not me. Not Dobe Yarnell. Not Dave Grande or Tom Gaddy. Not Logan Ware either, I'll gamble. Not anybody but this fool girl.'

Loren Rudd's first fear now changed to indignant anger. She lifted the quirt that had hung at her saddle horn. 'Let go of my rein,' she flared at Morry Seever. 'Let go or—'

Seever laughed, leaned over, and jerked the quirt from her hand with such violence as to numb her fingers. 'Had you hit me with this I'd have wound it around your pretty neck,' he leered.

Loren twisted in her saddle. 'Lister! Make this fool—'

She broke off, shocked at the look on Lister Beckwith's face. It was one of stark, livid fear. Now it was Fred Harmon who laughed.

'Save your breath, sister. Friend Beckwith ain't makin' anybody do anything. Ain't an ounce of wolf in him now—just all coyote.'

Loren turned to Mize Huncutt.

'You've no right,' she cried desperately, 'no

right at all to bother us.'

Huncutt did not even answer her. He swung his horse around and said to his men, 'Bring 'em along.'

In the next half hour Loren Rudd thought of many things. She thought of jumping out of her saddle and trying to run. She thought of trying to snatch her reins away from Morry Seever. She did neither because she realized it would do her no good to try. Finally she thought of the things Logan Ware had told her, warnings he had given her, and she went cold and shrinking inside.

Once she looked at Lister Beckwith, riding beside her, with Fred Harmon close at his heels. Beckwith would not meet her glance, just staring straight ahead. Beads of sweat stood out on his face. Loren felt a little sick at the utter fear she recognized. She looked swiftly away to where the bleak buildings of Guenoc began to lift out of the tawny range ahead.

Men came out on the ramshackle porch of the old stage station. Loren recognized Dobe Yarnell but not Dave Grande and Black Tom Gaddy, as she had never seen them before. But they were there.

Loren tried to keep her head high and meet the looks which came her way with cold, scornful dignity. She was able to do this until she stared into Dave Grande's cold black eyes. Then she looked away, flushing scarlet. Her flesh crawled.

'Mize,' said Grande, 'you sure drew a pair of aces this trip. Bring 'em in!'

Morry Seever said to Loren, 'You can get down and walk in like a lady, or I lug you in under my arm.'

Loren went in. The room was musty with stale tobacco smoke, with the stale dregs of whisky, with dust and heat and cobwebs. A round-backed chair was pushed toward Loren and she sank into it.

Mize Huncutt faced Lister Beckwith, feet spread, heavy jaw and shoulders pushed forward. Huncutt's eyes were little and cold and merciless.

'Got anything to say?' he growled.

Beckwith licked his lips. 'Only that I don't understand you fellows goin' tough and hostile like this. Anybody would think I'd tried to cut your throats.'

'Not quite that, maybe,' charged Huncutt. 'For your nerve wouldn't reach that far. But you've tried to double-cross us, which is just as bad. We had an agreement, Beckwith, you an' me an' Dobe an' Dave Grande. It was to be a four-way split of Hat when we got it chopped down to our size. We didn't have our fingers crossed when we made that deal. Maybe you did. It would seem so.'

'I don't know what you're talkin' about,' blurted Beckwith.

There was a harsh curse and Dave Grande caught Beckwith by the arm, whirling him around. 'You know damn well what Mize is talkin' about. But you weren't satisfied with just a share. You wanted it all, includin' the girl. A handy way to get all of Hat, wasn't it? Talk the girl into marryin' you and then move in on Hat as lord and master? Not that I blame you for wantin' the girl, though I doubt you wanted her as much as you wanted the Hat ranch. But the point is, you were aimin' to double-cross the rest of us, and that don't go! You should have realized that after you saw what happened to Tilton Bennett. Well?'

Loren didn't want to look at Lister Beckwith, but she couldn't help herself. It wasn't good to see in anyone what she saw in Beckwith at this moment. For she saw the guilt of him in his sweat-slimed face, in the workings of his lips, the twitching of his hands—saw guilt and a stupefying fear.

A vast shame overwhelmed her. Shame of Beckwith, shame of herself. She felt cheap, soiled. Out of nowhere the thought of Logan Ware flashed through her mind and she tried to picture him in Beckwith's place at this moment.

She knew what Ware's reaction to Grande's words would have been. He'd have had Grande by the throat, shaking the evil life out of him. Violence perhaps, but magnificent violence...

'What do you want me to do?' croaked Beckwith. 'I'll do anything you boys say. I'll get out of the valley. I'll—'

'All right,' cut in Grande. 'Get out!'

Mize Huncutt started to say something, but Grande cut him short with a glance. A relief, almost as sickening to watch as the fear which had convulsed him, showed in Lister Beckwith's face. He seemed to have forgotten Loren entirely. What lay ahead of her was of no apparent concern to him whatever, just so long as he got clear himself. He almost shambled in his hurry to leave the place.

Mize Huncutt spat on the floor. 'Old Draw Beckwith was at least half a man. But his son ...!' Huncutt spat again.

Black Tom Gaddy said, 'It's a mistake to let him go, Dave.'

Grande grinned evilly. 'I didn't want to mess up your floor, Tom. All right, Morry. And don't miss!'

Loren, dismayed and shaken by this sinister ending of what had started out as a casual ride across cheerful, sunlit range, was slow in getting Grande's intention. By the time she did it was too late.

For Morry Seever, tight and venomous, reached behind a door and brought out a Winchester rifle. At the first pound of hoofs as Lister Beckwith hit his saddle and started off, Seever stepped through the front door and raised the rifle. The move was as swift, precise, and deadly as a snake striking. The rifle steadied, then leaped in recoil, the hard blast of it running away in whipping echo.

Seever lowered the reeking weapon. 'I didn't miss,' he said with thin, callous satisfaction.

Cold horror held Loren motionless for a moment. Then she hit her feet, flaming.

'You cowardly, treacherous brutes! You filthy redhanded murderers! Logan Ware is right. He's been right all the time. Now at last I see and understand. You'll pay for this. You'll pay for everything. Logan will hunt you down, wipe you out. And once I doubted him—and my father. But they were right—right!'

Dave Grande turned on her, his eyes burning black and cruel.

'Don't get your hopes too high, my dear,' he mocked. 'Because your father's dead and Ware soon will be. We have plans for Mr Ware. He'll be taken care of shortly. So let's forget him just now and talk about you. They say it's a woman's privilege to change her mind. Well, you've changed yours several times, it seems. Now you're goin' to change it again.'

Loren's knees were shaking but she faced him and the loathing she poured out at him through direct and burning eyes brought dark blood to his face.

Grande took a swift step toward her, hand half lifted as though to strike. Dobe Yarnell's voice cut at him, harsh and blunt.

'Easy, Dave. That wouldn't do no good an' ain't what we're here for. Keep your hands off her!'

Grande whirled. 'You goin' soupy on us, too, Yarnell?'

Dobe Yarnell shrugged. 'You know better than that. But all I'm interested in is Hat cows an' Hat range. And in not havin' half a state clamorin' for my scalp when we get done what we've set out to do. We keep this fight for Hat strictly a man's fight an' nobody on the outside is goin' to bother us when it's done an' we've got what we've set out after. But should word get out of a girl bein' slapped around an' mistreated we'd have five counties gunnin' for us. How about that, Mize?'

Mize Huncutt looked Loren over with bleak and unsympathetic eyes. 'Depends,' he growled. 'Part ways you're right. Then again, things could depend on what we have to do to get her to sign things over to us. She wants to be sensible, I'm all for not touchin' a hair on her head. But should we have to get rough, why then ...!' He hunched his shoulders.

Dobe Yarnell said, 'I'll talk to her.'

He moved over beside Grande. Looking at Yarnell, Loren saw nothing calculated to give comfort. The man had not warned off Grande because of softened feelings toward her or because of the emergence of some gentler side of his nature. For there was not a gentle side to Dobe Yarnell. He was just being severely practical, weighing cause and effect and considering the future, and what it held for his interests.

'Once you were set to sign over part of Hat to Mize Huncutt an' me,' said Yarnell bluntly. 'You figgered it the right thing to do, then. You gave your word. Now you're tryin' to crawfish. It don't go. You'll stick to the original deal—or you'll take the consequences.' He glanced at Dave Grande.

'There never was any original deal,' retorted Loren, surprised at the steadiness of her voice. 'I said I was willing to consider certain claims against the Hat ranch and, if proven correct and just, to rectify them. I know now that they were lies, just as Logan Ware said they were. So I'll sign nothing. Even if I did, no fair court would consider such claims binding, if signed under threat and duress.'

'We'll worry about that court an' what it says later on,' Yarnell said.

'I'll sign nothing,' repeated Loren.

Dave Grande cursed. 'You see, Yarnell? Let me handle this.'

Again the look which Grande bent on her made Loren's flesh crawl. 'Something for you to understand,' he said harshly. 'I got as much at stake as any man here, maybe more. There's no sentimental mush in me. You'll do as you're told, or wish you'd never been born. We'll draw up the necessary claims right now and you'll sign them. Understand?'

Loren had to draw on all her courage to face him. 'Anything I signed now would be worthless.'

Grande made a violent, impatient gesture. 'Like Yarnell said, we'll worry about the courts later.'

'There is something you don't know,' went on Loren coolly. 'While my father did leave the Hat ranch to me in his will, he later had drawn up certain provisions that had to be fulfilled before the will would become valid.'

'You're lying, stalling for time,' rapped Grande. 'And my patience is running out.'

Now it was Mize Huncutt, shrewd and scheming, who took a hand.

'Wait a minute, Dave.' Huncutt looked at Loren. 'These provisions you speak of—did Tilton Bennett know about them?'

'Not directly, so far as I know,' answered Loren honestly. 'But I think he probably suspected something of the sort, which was why he came out to Hat and tried to make a deal with Logan Ware.'

'The damned, double-dealing whelp!' snapped Grande harshly. 'Well, he got his needings.'

'Right both ways, Dave,' nodded Mize Huncutt. 'Yet here's something we better think about. Crooked as he was, there's one thing you couldn't take away from Bennett. He knew the law and how to get around it if any man ever did. The point is this. If Bennett suspected an angle of law that couldn't be cracked, an angle so strong he was willin' to take his chances at double-crossin' us, you can bet that angle is plenty strong. Let's consider things a mite.'

'Just what are these provisions?' demanded Dobe Yarnell.

'Why,' answered Loren, 'that I must live a full year at Hat before the original will takes effect. During that year I have no authority at all over Hat affairs. I can neither buy nor sell, hire nor fire, nor make commitments of any kind. Only one person may do this.'

'Logan Ware?' snarled Dave Grande.

'Logan Ware.'

Grande went into a fury of cursing. The man's cold, unemotional front had disappeared entirely. All the venomous malignancy in his make-up was loose and stalking now.

The others waited him out, then Mize Huncutt said, 'The girl's givin' us the truth, for it explains Tilton Bennett's switch-over. So there's plans we got to toss out an' new plans we got to make. We got to move strong and hard and fast—and for keeps. Gaddy, take the girl upstairs an' lock her in one of them rooms. Dave, quit that useless cussin'. Let's get down to cold turkey.'

The stairs were steep and shaky with age. Loren climbed them slowly, Black Tom Gaddy stamping along behind. She had no idea of what lay ahead for her, but of two things she was sure. Any chance of escape at the moment was impossible. And just so she could get away by herself for a time, away from Dave Grande's wicked eyes and the crass leers of Morry Seever and others like him.

The room was small, hot, stifling with dead air and ancient dust. There was a battered old iron bunk and a chair minus one arm and shaky from missing rungs.

The door closed behind her, the lock snicked. Black Tom Gaddy's steps retreated down the musty hall.

There was a single window and Loren crossed to it. One of the upper panes was broken out. The whole thing looked flimsy. But this was a second-story window and the drop from it to the ground was high and sheer. Just the same, come night, if a person was desperate enough, she might chance that drop...

Until then there was nothing a person could do but wait. Loren sat gingerly on the edge of the bunk and began to shake. She clenched her hands together, squeezed them tightly between her knees. Still they shook.

She thought of Lister Beckwith and how he had died. She thought of Dave Grande and his scorching eyes, and shudder after shudder convulsed her.

Then she thought of Logan Ware and the tears came, and through quivering lips she whispered his name, over and over.

CHAPTER TWELVE

CRIMSON HOURS

Powder-blue twilight lay over Long Valley when Logan Ware and Slide Maidlie rode back to Hat headquarters. The rest of the outfit was already there and Tex Fortune was out at the corrals, waiting. Tex looked harsh.

'Better swap to fresh broncs,' he said grimly. 'We got work ahead. Mother Sutton was just talking to me. The girl's gone.'

'Gone!' Ware, just stepped from his saddle, whirled on Tex as though stung with a whiplash.

'She went off ridin' with Lister Beckwith hours ago. She hasn't come back. That Beckwith hombre! I knew he was all skunk.'

For a moment Ware stood stock-still, trying to get the import of this. Something seemed to close about his heart, cold and strangling. Then he shook himself. 'I'll see Mother Sutton.'

He found her frankly worried.

'Loren and Beckwith left not long after the rest of you boys pulled out,' Mother Sutton explained. 'I'd been talking with her, trying to make her understand why Chain Kelsey had to be hung. I didn't get very far with her. She seemed very distant and bitter. Then Lister

Beckwith showed up and Loren went off with him.'

Ware had full hold on himself again. 'She's threatened once or twice to go back to town to live. Maybe this time she has. Then again, maybe she and Beckwith rode a little further than usual and are just late getting back. If they don't show up by the time supper's done with, we'll start a search.'

In the cook house hungry men ate and reported on the day's patrol to Ware. Most of the borders of Hat range had been ridden out and no untoward activity of any kind seen, no massing of more Flat Y and Block H cattle along Hat borders, no suspicious prowlers.

Ware ate with one ear cocked for the sound of hoofs which would have signaled the arrival of Loren Rudd and Lister Beckwith. But none came, so Ware began giving orders for the search. Then it was Slide Maidlie who spoke up.

'I'm not aimin' to butt in,' he said. 'But I got a queer feelin' about this thing. Mebbe Miss Loren has just decided to stay in town, like you say she might. Then again, mebbe she's ridden into something. Let's remember what happened last night. You threw a little soiree against Mize Huncutt's headquarters. You cleaned up a couple of sour spots in town. You advertised the fact that Hat was ready and able to ride and smash and not wait around any more to be raw-hided before hitting back. Right?'

'Correct,' Ware said impatiently. 'But what's that got to do with Loren Rudd being gone?'

'Mebbe they got her. Huncutt, Yarnell—that crowd. They know we'll ride in a search. Supposing they draw all of us away from headquarters? Then they come in, grab Hat headquarters while we're gone. We're in a tough spot. They'd have the girl, have Hat. They'd be fixed to force a pretty good trade for themselves. How about it, Tex?'

'You got an angle there,' admitted Tex gravely. 'For that matter, you and me and Logan can make a search in this case just as well as the whole outfit could. Better in some ways, for we can travel faster and with a lot less noise and fuss. Logan, I think Slide is making sense. Think on it.'

Ware had a lot of respect for Maidlie's opinions. The gunman had had wide experience with the devious schemings of men. And Tex was right in his contention that three of them could travel faster and more quietly than a larger number could.

'All right,' he said. 'Tex and Slide and me will see what we can find. If we don't turn up a trail by daylight tomorrow, the whole outfit gets into it. And in case Slide is guessing right, the rest of you be on your toes tonight. Rainy, you take charge. Put guards out.'

Ware, Maidlie, and Tex headed for town.

Ware said, 'If we have no luck in Canyon we'll hit Beckwith's Two Stirrup headquarters. If that is empty we'll prowl Block H and Flat Y. There should be sign somewhere.'

Canyon lay quiet, Lake Street a channel of darkness, splashed here and there with lights from window and door. Logan Ware pulled in at Dub Pennymaker's stable, saying, 'Dub generally knows what goes on in town. I'll ask him if he's seen Loren.'

Ware could not raise Dub anywhere about the stable, which was dark and quiet.

'Look in the harness room,' suggested Tex. 'Dub may have turned in early tonight.'

Ware opened the door and the room was black dark and seemingly empty. He was about to turn away when he heard a low, muttering groan. 'Somebody in here,' he said to Tex over his shoulder.

Tex and Slide Maidlie crowded in behind him. Ware scratched a match and in the thin flare looked down on the securely tied figure stretched on the bunk. Tex, peering over Ware's shoulder, swore in some wonder.

'Milo Kron! Now how in billy hell did he get here?'

'By the looks of it,' answered Ware slowly, 'somebody hit him over the head and then tied him up, hand and foot. He's beginning to grunt a little, but he's still out. He'll keep. Let's keep prowling.'

They went out, gave the black street a long,

careful survey. Ware said, 'Stubby Hoffmeyer may know something. We'll try the hotel first and then the Empire.'

They went along the street, leading their horses. Slide Maidlie murmured, 'This night's got a feel to it. Watch yourselves!'

They halted back from the reaching lights of the hotel, keened the night again. Ware said, 'We're gettin' jumpy as old women. Wait here. I'll see Stubby.'

He ducked under the hitch rail and climbed the hotel steps into the open light flare of the wide door. And at that moment the night shook under the bellow of heavy gun report.

Ware's reaction was explosive and swift. In one long, whirling leap he was out of that dangerous light and flattened against the darkness of the hotel wall. There was the trample of hoofs as the startled horses swung and reared. Slide Maidlie and Tex Fortune spun and crouched, guns drawn and ready. A moment of breathless silence fell.

'You all right, Logan?' rapped Tex. 'I didn't hear no slug.'

'Nothin' came my way,' Ware answered. 'I don't get this. That shot wasn't at me.'

Now it was Dub Pennymaker's voice that came out of the dark, over past the corner of the hotel.

'Out here, Logan—out here! No need of worryin' now. I fixed this coyote—plenty!'

They went over there and found Dub

Pennymaker standing, a dim figure in the thin starlight.

'What goes on, Dub?' demanded Ware.

'He was aimin' to get you, Logan. But I got him first,' answered Dub. 'This is somethin' I been promisin' myself ever since he rode that Cherry bronc of mine an' then beat me up. I swore then that I'd get even. Come an' get him if you want him. It's Fred Harmon.'

The heavy rumble of the gunshot had stirred up the usual excitement and a crowd began to gather. Somebody brought a lantern and the glow of it showed old Dub, cold and grim of face, with an ancient Sharps buffalo gun across his arm. Dub made no apologies.

'I see Harmon an' Milo Kron come sneakin' into town just about dark,' he explained. 'There was somethin' about 'em that made me wonder, somethin' like they was fixin to rob a bank or pull some kinda dirty business. So I got this old buff gun of mine an' kept a eye on 'em. By 'n by they split up, Harmon headin' off upstreet toward the hotel, while Kron, he comes sneakin' into my stable. I don't mess around none with Kron. I jest snooker back in the dark an' when he comes by I larrup him over the head with the barrel of my gun. Then I tied him up an' stowed him away in my harness room. After which I injun out after Harmon.'

Dub paused a moment, lifted his thin shoulders a little straighter.

'I locate Harmon hid out where he could

watch the hotel door. I couldn't figger exactly jest what he was up to, but I know'd it was somethin' damn shady. So I set myself to watch him. Nothin' happened until you come along, Logan. The second you showed up agin the light from Stubby Hoffmeyer's door yonder, Harmon set to pull down on you with that carbine layin' under him. Right then I let him have it. An' I feel like a whole man again for the first time since he mistreated Cherry an' give me that beatin'. I dunno how the rest of you feel about it, but me, I'm plumb satisfied.'

Stubby Hoffmeyer, in the forefront of the crowd, said, 'You did a first-rate job, Dub. I'm for you, all the way.'

Ware dropped a hand on Dub's shoulder. 'Them who ask for it end up gettin' it, old-timer. I owe you plenty for this. But tell me somethin'. Did you see Miss Rudd in town today?'

'Never did, Logan.'

Ware turned to Stubby Hoffmeyer. 'How about you, Stubby? Did Miss Rudd show up at your hotel?'

'Ain't seen her since she went out to Hat to live, Logan,' answered Stubby.

Ware said, 'Come on, Dub—Tex—Slide. I want to talk to Kron.'

At the stable Dub lighted a lantern. Milo Kron had come fully back to his senses and blinked stupidly upward as the lantern light spread across his face. Some of the curious crowd had followed down to the stable, but Tex Fortune held them outside.

'This is Hat business,' he said curtly. 'And none of yours.'

Ware looked down at Milo Kron and his voice held a raw edge as he spoke. 'Hear that gun go off about five minutes ago, Kron?'

Kron nodded heavily. 'I heard it,' he mumbled.

'That shot killed Fred Harmon. He was layin' for me but a friend of mine beat him to it. You and Harmon didn't come to town to pull this job of your own free will. Somebody sent you. Who did?'

Kron rolled his head in hopeless desperation.

'They can't whip you, Ware. Your damned luck runs too strong. They move this way they come out worst. They move that way they come out the same. I've had enough. What do I get if I talk?'

'The question,' said Ware remorselessly, 'is what you get if you don't talk. You're in no spot to bargain. The tree that held Chain Kelsey will hold you if you want it that way. I'm in no mood to waste time arguing. You talk and talk fast and straight.'

For a brief moment the light of stubbornness began to build up in Kron's eyes. Then it went out of him, leaving him dry-lipped and sweating.

'All right,' he croaked, 'you win. If it's the

girl you're lookin' for, Dave Grande an' Black Tom Gaddy got her out at Guenoc. An' if you want to keep Hat from bein' taken over you better have your crew all at headquarters an' plenty on their toes.'

'Tonight?' snapped Ware.

'Tonight. Huncutt an' Yarnell are goin' to hit Hat all out with their combined outfits. They figger the place will be empty, with all hands out lookin' for that girl.'

Without looking at Maidlie, Ware said, 'Slide, you're the smartest fox I know. Call Tex in.'

Tex came in and Ware told him what Kron had said. He added, 'Hit for the ranch, Tex—and fast! Get the boys set. When Huncutt and Yarnell show, give 'em what for.'

'That,' growled Tex, 'is a pleasure I been lookin' forward to for a long time. You an' Slide headin' for Guenoc?'

'Right! Get going.'

Tex hurried out.

Kron said, 'They sent me an' Harmon to town to lay for you, Ware. They figgered you'd probably look here first for the girl.'

'Sweet crowd!' drawled Slide Maidlie softly. 'With you done for, Logan—and with them holding the girl and getting physical control of Hat, the story would just about been told. Morning would have seen a big change in Long Valley.'

'Morning will still see a big change,' declared

Ware grimly. 'Kron, how did they get Miss Rudd out to Guenoc? Did Beckwith toll her out there?'

'No. Huncutt picked up her an' Beckwith out on the open range. They were ridin' around gay as you please when Mize an' some of the rest of us bumped into them. Mize an' Yarnell an' Grande figgered it a big break of luck for us. I can see where it was anything but that, now. The luck is all yours, Ware.'

'Beckwith—what about him? Once he was in this just as deep as Huncutt and the others.'

'Yeah, he was. Then he set out to play a lone hand, aimin' to marry the girl an' get all of Hat for himself. Leastways, that's how Huncutt an' the others figgered. He paid heavy for the double-cross. He's dead now. Grande had Morry Seever gun him.'

The bleakness in Ware's face deepened. 'Grande seems to figure pretty prominent in all these schemes. How come?'

'Ain't you got that figgered? Grande is the big wolf of the crowd. Has been, right from the first. He owns more of the Flat Y than Dobe Yarnell does, an' he's half-an-half pardners with Mize Huncutt. They've kept the tie-ups pretty quiet. Now—what about me?'

'That depends. On how much of this you've told us turns out to be the truth. If you haven't lied, you'll get your break. If you have, well, that cottonwood tree will be waiting.' Ware turned to Dub Pennymaker.

'Can you hold him here until tomorrow, Dub?'

'I'll hold him until hell freezes,' promised Dub stoutly. 'He'll be here when you want him, Logan.'

Ware looked at Maidlie. 'You and me to Guenoc, Slide?'

'You'd go alone if I didn't say yes,' drawled the gunman. 'But I wouldn't miss this for a spotted bronc. Got a couple of debts to pay. One to Miss Loren because she's been good to me. And one to Mr Dave Grande, for other reasons. Are Grande an' Gaddy alone at Guenoc, Kron?'

'Orcutt and Seever were to stay there with 'em, just in case.'

'That,' said Ware, 'is all we want to know. Come on, Slide.'

From town they rode fast but with caution, wary of possible trail guards or other night riders who might carry an alarm ahead of them to Guenoc. It was hard for Ware to use this caution. Milo Kron's blurted story had filled him with a wild bitter fury and anxiety. He was forcing himself to keep this fury under control, to make it a cold and settled flame, for this was a time for clear thinking as well as ruthless action.

He kept thinking of Loren Rudd, of her fine cleanness of mind and purpose. Mistaken though some of her ideas had been, Ware knew that she was honest in them, just as she would always be honest in all things. It was not her fault that she had been unable to discard these ideas readily, for they were the products of a lifetime of influence by a well-intentioned but mistaken mother who had never been able to understand the realities of Hampton Rudd's bid for a cattle empire.

Yet there were times when the influence of her father's blood had come to the fore in the girl. There was discernible in her a growing receptiveness to the spell of the open range, to the vigor and purpose of control of wide acres, of cattle herds, of awakening pride in and for the Hat ranch. Given time, Ware was certain she would understand and grasp the meaning of Hat in full.

But now—now this last and most vicious exhibition of the violence which had repelled her. Captured and held against her will by such as Dave Grande, Black Tom Gaddy, and others. Lister Beckwith, whom she had mistakenly believed in, shot down, perhaps right before her eyes. If she hated Long Valley and all that was in it now, no one could really blame her.

The miles had rolled back while Ware mused grimly over his thoughts. Now Slide Maidlie's slow drawl broke in.

'We better leave the broncs here, boy, and go in on foot. Hoofbeats, even at a slow walk, carry far on a night like this.'

Ware looked across the night. A single light,

like a furtive eye, yellow and malignant, peered back at him. All about the dark pressed down, still and vast. But that was Guenoc out there, not over half a mile away now. And Slide Maidlie was right.

Ware reined in and stepped from his saddle. He stripped off his spurs and hung them on his saddle horn, Maidlie doing the same. From his saddle scabbard Ware drew his rifle, cradled it across his arm.

'We'll swing off the main trail and injun in,' said Maidlie.

They prowled down the dark distance, stopping every now and then to search the night with alert and straining senses. In time the black bulk of the stage station buildings lifted and grew solid before them. That single light glowed on, a watchful, sinister orb.

Now Ware and Maidlie were but crouched and soft stealing shadows. At every step they half expected a challenge or alarm to crash across the poised and waiting silence. The breathless tension pulled their nerves to a hard, keen edge.

Once when they paused Slide Maidlie murmured, 'It may be exactly like Kron said, but then again maybe the setup has changed since Kron and Harmon left for town. We may bump into more guns than we think. Either way, once we start, speed will be the main thing. For there's no telling about a snake like Dave Grande. Cornered, with the black ace lookin' him in the eye, he might hit at the girl. And it would be small comfort to us to smoke him down, if he'd thrown a shot at Miss Loren first. This is for keeps, boy!'

'Yeah,' gritted Ware. 'For keeps!'

Abruptly they went down, flat on their faces. For, from out behind the station buildings, where the old corrals stood, came a dark surge of riders, nearly a score of them. For a moment Ware thought he and Maidlie had been spotted and these riders were racing to ride them down. Instinct screamed at him to rise and go to work with his rifle. But Slide Maidlie's hand on his arm steadied him, held him quiet.

The riders pounded past them, so close that the churned-up dust was an acrid, invisible cloud to sting their eyes and lay a bitter flavor in their nostrils and throats. They never moved until the last echo of hoofs had faded down the dark distance.

There was no mistaking now the mission of that group of riders. The preciseness of their direction told that. There rode the combined forces of the Flat Y and the Block H. Mize Huncutt and Dobe Yarnell were away for the surprise attack and planned capture of Hat headquarters. Milo Kron had not lied.

'Lucky we decided to leave our broncs back south a distance,' murmured Maidlie. 'Else we'd have ridden right into the middle of that crowd. Well, there rides the big play for Hat, Logan. One thing, Tex has had plenty of time to reach headquarters and get set. Tex is a pretty wise old juniper. He'll have a right smart reception cooked up for that crowd.'

So now they went on, caution redoubled as they cut the distance down. That yellow eye of light now became the rectangle of a window. Ware stopped Maidlie and whispered the layout of the place to him, for this was the gunman's first visit to Guenoc. There was a door, Ware told him, the main door, just to the left of that lighted window, a door that was closed now and which opened inward.

In whispers they debated the advisability of attack from the rear of the place, but discarded this as it would mean blind, dark fumbling through strange rooms before they could reach the barroom where the light lived. Their best chance, they decided, was sudden, smashing attack from the front, basing their chance of success on surprise and fast shooting.

It was legitimate to believe surprise would be on their side. For Grande wouldn't know of the happenings in town. He wouldn't know that Fred Harmon was dead, that Milo Kron had talked. It was legitimate to feel that Grande would believe all of the Hat crew riding far and wide in search of Loren Rudd, suspecting many things but hardly that she would be held at Guenoc by him.

For all Logan Ware knew, Grande would reason, he had skipped the country as he'd been ordered to. Nor would Ware know that in this plot for the overthrow of Hat, he, Dave Grande, was the main instigator, and that Black Tom Gaddy was in on it too.

These, Ware reasoned, could be Dave Grande's conclusions and in whispered words he outlined them to Slide Maidlie, who murmured in reply, 'As good reasonin' as any. We'll base our play on it.'

They cut the distance between them and the buildings to a hundred yards, to fifty yards. Abruptly the door of the place opened and against the light the hulking figure of Spade Orcutt loomed.

He had a rifle across one arm. He paused there a moment, listening to a remark made by someone in the room behind him, and gave growling answer to it. Then he closed the door and the ancient boards of the porch creaked under his stride. His head and shoulders loomed momentarily against the light of the window, then passed into the darkness beyond. Chair legs grated and rawhide lacings creaked under the bulk of a sitting man's weight.

So that was that. Spade Orcutt was settled in a chair as guard and lookout against the blackness of that hostile wall. This did not make the task of Logan Ware and Slide Maidlie any simpler.

Ware and Maidlie had no need to trade whispered conferences any longer. Both understood fully what had to be done. They went in inch by inch, foot by foot. Their rifles they left in the dust behind them. This would be six-gun work, close and fast.

Twenty yards from the edge of the porch. Ten yards...

Then, dull and brutish as he was, Spade Orcutt knew the stirrings of animal instinct against danger. They heard him shift uneasily, heard the small, metallic snick as he drew back the hammer of his rifle. These sounds placed him.

Slide Maidlie said, 'Now!'

They shot almost together, Ware and Maidlie did. The combined roar of report splintered the breathless, waiting quiet of the night like a thunder blast. Then they were up, up and rushing in, ducking under the hitch rail.

Spade Orcutt, cut through and through by two heavy slugs, staggered blindly to the edge of the porch, off it and against the hitch rail, over which he jackknifed and hung, limply.

Ware and Maidlie crossed the porch in long leaps, smashed into the door, their combined weight almost tearing it off the hinges as it crashed open. Then, before the deadly roll of guns began a final tolling, clear and sharp and brief as the flicker of a camera shutter they saw the lighted room and what it held.

Three men had been at a table with cards between them and whisky glasses at their elbows. Dave Grande, Black Tom Gaddy, and Morry Seever.

Seever, small, tight, venomous, was reacting

with the speed of a striking snake. He was out of his chair, had a gun drawn and flaming all in one move. The blare of the weapon was straight at Logan Ware and the shock of the bullet spun Ware half around, his left arm and shoulder going numb. But Ware shot across his turning body before Seever could chop down a second time.

Seever, still moving, seemed to abruptly strike an invisible, immovable obstacle. He put a foot which appeared to be exploring for some dark and substanceless support and, finding none, buckled under him. Then he fell, loosely.

It seemed strange to hear Slide Maidlie laughing, between the first and second shots he threw, lightning fast. But Maidlie was laughing at Dave Grande, laughing without mirth. For into Grande's black, cold eyes had leaped the stupefying realization that here before him was the black ace of death, that here was the end of all plans, all scheming, all of everything.

These things lay stark and naked in the look of him while Black Tom Gaddy died swiftly under the unerring smash of Slide Maidlie's first slug. Then the second slug ripped into Grande, knocking him half out of his chair.

At the far end of the bar a narrow stairway led upward, upward, to some second-story region of the place. And Dave Grande, recovering from the first drive of Maidlie's lead, made for these stairs in a lurching stagger, drawing a gun as he went.

It was a strange and bloodcurdling thing, this move of Grande's. He seemed to have forgotten Logan Ware and Slide Maidlie. His purpose was to climb those stairs and in the obsession of his last malignant move he made no attempt to throw a shot at either of them.

He was dying on his feet but he got to the third step before he shook and wavered under the combined impact of lead from the thudding guns of Ware and Maidlie. Then, of a sudden, the dark, poisonous spirit ran out of him. He fell against the slope of the stairs, turned partly over, and slid down them to the floor, where he lay, a huddled, lifeless shape.

Silence that was almost explosive settled momentarily down. Then Maidlie said, 'I told you it would be that way, boy. We'll find Miss Loren somewhere beyond those stairs.'

Ware stepped over Grande and climbed into the utter dark of the narrow hallway above, a hall full of trapped heat and musty air. He staggered a little, bewildered at the effort it cost him to make the climb and at the weaving unevenness of this hall floor. He dropped his gun, got a sulphur match from his pocket, scratched it to a small, flickering flame.

A door loomed on his right, open and black. Ware lurched through it, holding the match high. The room was empty. He spun into the hall again, saw another door, closed this time. The match flickered out. Ware threw his right shoulder against the locked portal, heard it creak and protest.

'Loren!' he called. 'Loren ...!' His voice was heavy in his throat, thick and hoarse.

He heard her answer, small at first, then with a rising, growing note of relief and joy. 'Here—in here. Logan—Logan Ware ...!'

He reeled back, then smashed the door again. Ancient wood splintered and he was through, falling to one knee.

'Loren!' he mumbled again.

Then the floor jumped up and smashed him in the face and everything trailed off into black, swirling shadows.

CHAPTER THIRTEEN

ONE MAN'S FAITH

All was dark and quiet at Hat headquarters. Tex Fortune had been urging Mother Sutton to take the ranch buckboard and ride into Canyon for the night.

'It's goin' to be pretty rough when Huncutt and Yarnell hit, ma'am,' warned Tex. 'Me and the boys would all feel better if we knew you was plumb safe and away from any chance lead.'

Mother Sutton would hear none of this. 'I'll be safe enough,' she declared. 'You're forgetting, Tex, that the walls of this ranch house are of stone. Besides, someone is sure to be hurt and then I'll be needed. I wish I could be as sure of Loren Rudd's safety as I am of my own.'

'If any two men in the world can get that girl clear, Logan Ware and Slide Maidlie are the two,' said Tex. 'Logan said that this night would settle a lot of things in Long Valley. I reckon he was right, ma'am. I still wish you'd head for town.'

'Nonsense!' Then Mother Sutton smiled at him. 'I'm of the old West too, Tex. Our generation never did run from a fight.'

Tex inclined his grizzled head in grave courtesy. 'I was forgettin' that. My apologies, ma'am. But please ma'am, put out all lights an' stay away from windows.'

Leaving the ranch house, Tex made the rounds. He had spread his all too thin forces to the most strategic advantage in key positions about headquarters. To all of them he had given the same advice.

'In a night fight the closer a man can get to the ground the safer he is. An' besides, that way you got a chance to get the other feller against the stars. He makes a better target then. Huncutt an' Yarnell are makin' this raid in the belief they'll find Hat jest about deserted, with all hands out lookin' for Miss Loren. We don't want to spoil that belief until we get 'em bunched and right where we want 'em. Then they get it. Don't open up until you hear me yell. We'll have just one light goin', which will be in the cookshack. That'll make 'em think that Smoky is holdin' the fort alone. But Smoky won't be in the cookshack. He'll be hunkered down at the far end of the corrals. You'll have to do without smokin' until this thing is over. Good luck!'

Tex had sent Joe and Speck Larribee out as scouts. They drifted in out of the dark abruptly. 'Pull in your belts,' announced Speck laconically. 'They're out there.'

The minutes grew full of slow, beating tension. Tex worked over to Smoky Atwater's side. 'They'll probably throw a round of lead to sort of test things,' Tex growled. 'Then if the reaction is right they'll come in a-hellin'. We'll give 'em the reaction. You get down to the cookshack. When they open up, Smoky, you blow out that light an' then do some yellin', like you was all alone an' mad an' scared. When they pile in, you know what to do.'

Smoky dodged away through the night. He had barely reached the cookshack when the rippling blast gunfire whipped in from the dark, lead smashing and thudding into wall and casement. Smoky blew out the light, darted out into the dark, and his yell echoed.

'Who's shootin'? You crazy damn fools—lay off that shootin'! You darn near hit me. Lay off that shootin'...!'

This was the only reply to that testing volley and it served the purpose Tex calculated it would. There sounded the pound of suddenly racing hoofs and Mize Huncutt and Dobe Yarnell led their combined crew toward what appeared easy conquest of Hat headquarters.

They clattered into the open compound between ranch house and corrals and Dobe Yarnell's voice lifted harshly. 'Couple of you get down to the cookshack an' take care of that cook. The rest of you stay put until Mize an' me look through the ranch house. Allus did want a good look at Hamp Rudd's fancy hangout.'

'Wrong time, Yarnell!' came Tex Fortune's mocking voice from the dark. Then Tex lifted a shrill yell. With the yell he was shooting.

Joe and Speck Larribee from beside the bunkhouse in the deep blackness there. Rainy Day from one corner of the ranch house and Packy Maroon from another. Curly Russell and Ed Morlan by the saddle shed. Tex Fortune and Smoky Atwater from the corrals.

They opened up with bleak and bitter purpose. Dobe Yarnell never realized his ambition to see the inside of the Hat ranch house. A bullet from that first defensive volley struck him just under the heart.

It wasn't a matter of minutes but of seconds. Barely thirty of them. In those few measured watch ticks the future of Long Valley was settled for all time. Horses went down, riders went down. There was hardly any return fire and what there was of this was panic-stricken, desperate, and completely wild. Survivors raced madly away into the night, leadership gone, purpose broken. The spirit of Hamp Rudd was stalking this night, holding what he had built, guaranteeing its enduring future.

When it was all over with they found Mize Huncutt spread-eagled in the very center of the compound.

It was a good three weeks later that Logan Ware got out of his own bunk at Hat headquarters. Slide Maidlie and Tex Fortune helped him dress. They had to loop his shirt over his left arm and shoulder, stiff with bandages.

Tex was cussing him gruffly.

'Doc Abbey said you'd ought to stick to the blankets for at least another week. But you can be the damnedest, most bullheaded hombre...!'

'If I stayed in bed another minute I'd be loco as a jay bird,' retorted Ware. 'Anybody would think I'd really sopped up some lead instead of havin' just a smidgin little hole through my shoulder.'

'Huh!' snorted Tex. 'It ain't the hole so much as it is the blood that came out of it. You lost enough to supply three men. Well, it's your funeral. If you go all weak an' wobbly an' fall on your stubborn mug, remember I warned you. Hey, Slide?'

Slide Maidlie grinned. 'You warned him, Tex. But he seems to be doin' pretty good.'

Ware stood in the doorway of the bunkhouse, looking across the open, sun-swept interval between it and the ranch house. Empty, peaceful, and still was that spread of honest earth now. But there had been one savage night...

Over in back of the ranch house Mother Sutton was gathering a basket of snowy wash off a line. She looked at Ware gravely as he came slowly up.

'Is this wise, boy?' she asked gently. 'You gave us some anxious moments you know.'

Ware grinned. 'Gettin' stronger by the minute. Where's Loren?'

'Up at the burying ground, I think. She's been doing a lot of caring for her father's grave, lately.'

Ware started out that way, thinking how good the sun felt on his bared head, how the warmth of it beat through and brought comfort to his healing shoulder. A little breeze came running up the valley, a small, lazy breeze, friendly and sweet with the breath of space and sunshine. Ware turned his face to it and let it wash all through him.

Then he saw her, coming down the slope toward him, her fair hair shining in the sun. Concern was in her eyes and a gentle scolding on her lips.

'Foolish man! Do you want to be flat on your back again?'

He looked at her so long and steadily she

colored warmly. But her eyes held honest and marvelously soft.

'Only one thing I want,' he said. 'You. I reckon you've known that for a long time, Loren, but I wanted to say it and find out if there was any hope for me. We've seen rough times together, you and me, but that's all past and done with now. And you've got your ranch as you would want it to be, peaceful and quiet and safe.'

'Yes,' she said. 'I have. And what gave it to me? One man's faith. Yours. You kept faith with my father, you kept faith with me, with your friends, your crew, and yourself.'

She came steadily closer as she spoke, smiling very wisely. 'Remember that night at the patio entrance? Well, this makes us even.'

She cupped his face in both soft palms, pulled it down, and kissed him.

Matt Stuart was the byline used by L. P. Holmes on a number of outstanding Western novels. Born in a snowed-in log cabin in the heart of the Rockies near Breckenridge Colorado in 1895, Holmes moved with his family when very young to northern California and it was here that his father and older brothers built the ranch house where Holmes grew up and where, in later life, he would live again. He published his first story—'The Passing of the Ghost'—in Action Stories (9/25). He was paid ½¢ a word and received a check for $40. 'Yeah—forty bucks,' he said later. 'Don't laugh. In those far-off days ... a pair of young parents with a three-year-old son could buy a lot of groceries on forty bucks.' He went on to contribute nearly 600 stories of varying lengths to the magazine market as well as to write over fifty Western novels under his own name and as Matt Stuart. For the many years of his life, Holmes would write in the mornings and spend his afternoons calling on a group of friends in town, among them the blind Western author Charles H. Snow whom Lew Holmes always called 'Judge' Snow (because he was Napa's Justice of the Peace 1920–1924) and who frequently makes an appearance in later novels as a local justice in Holmes's imaginary Western communities. Holmes's Golden Age as an author was from 1948 through 1960. During these years under his Matt Stuart byline he produced such notable novels as *Dusty Wagons*, *Gunlaw at Vermillion*, *Wire in the Wind*, *Sunset Rider*, and *Gun Smoke Showdown*. This last was reprinted in paperback under the title *Saddle-Man*. In these novels one finds the themes so basic to his Western fiction: the loyalty which unites one man to another, the pride one must take in his work and a job well done, the innate generosity of most of the people who live in Holmes's ambient Western communities, and the vital relationship between a man and a woman in making a better life.

We hope you have enjoyed this Large Print book. Other Chivers Press or G.K. Hall & Co. Large Print books are available at your library or directly from the publishers.

For more information about current and forthcoming titles, please call or write, without obligation, to:

Chivers Press Limited
Windsor Bridge Road
Bath BA2 3AX
England
Tel. (01225) 335336

OR

G.K. Hall & Co.
P.O. Box 159
Thorndike, Maine 04986
USA
Tel. (800) 223–2336

All our Large Print titles are designed for easy reading, and all our books are made to last.